Other books by John D. Carter

Intelligence and Attention

Intimacy in Cocktail Lounges

Cape Lazo

Crazy Cousins

Belle Islet Lady

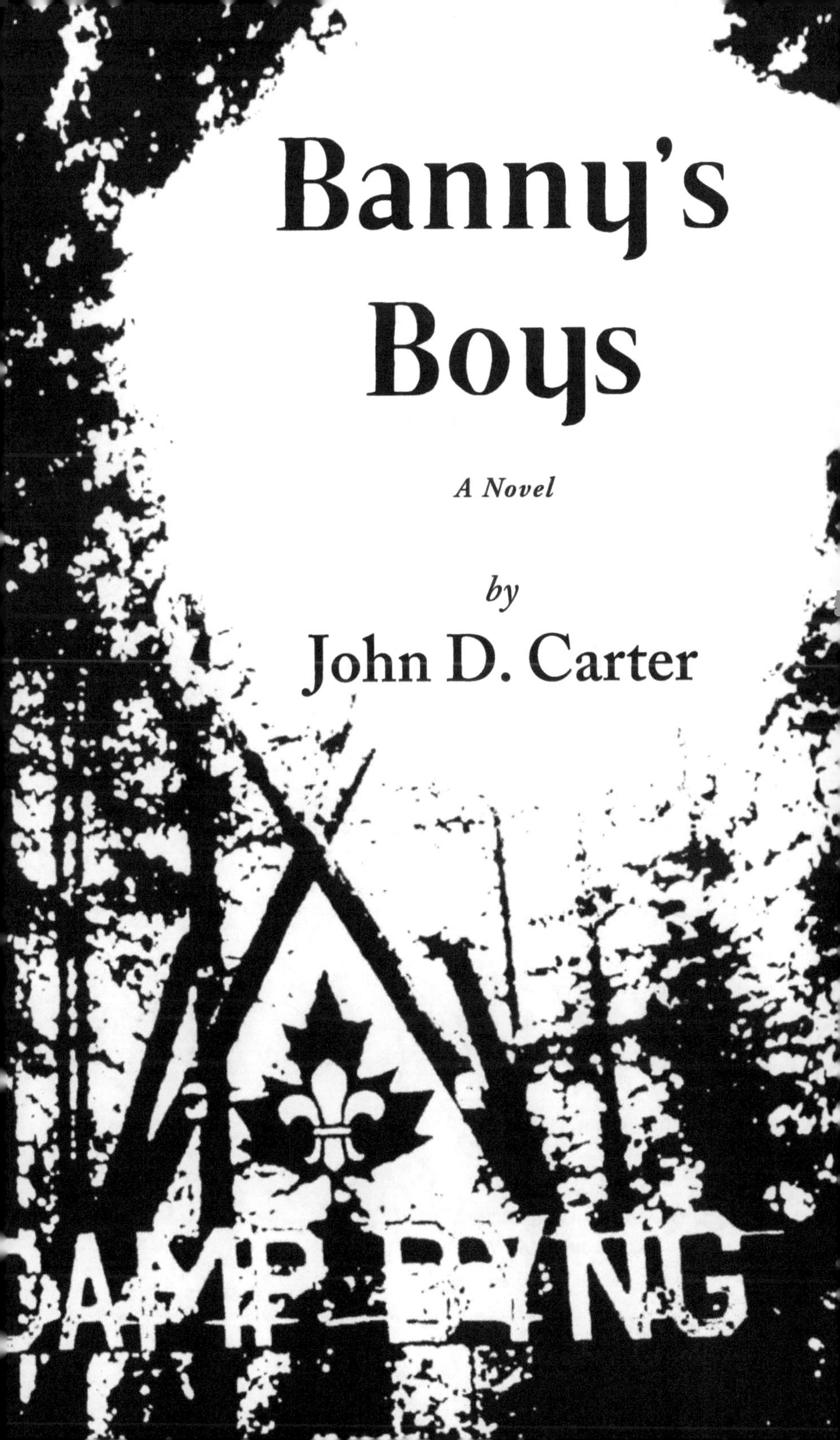

Banny's
Boys

A Novel

by

John D. Carter

Cover imagery:
"Camp Byng trees" ⓒ 2017, via Google Maps
Used under Creative Commons License v4.0.

Cover and Book Design: Vladimir Verano, Third Place Press

PUBLISHED BY

John D. Carter.

Belle.Islet@gmail.com

ISBN: 978-0-9940346-6-3

Designed by Third Place Press
Lake Forest Park, Washington
www.thirdplacepress.com

"Those we love do not go away, they walk beside us everyday."

~Dr. Randal Reilly

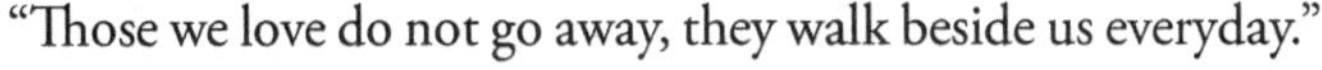

"When life gives you a hundred reasons to cry, show life you have a thousand reasons to smile."

~Shane Bighill

TABLE OF CONTENTS

Part One

Camp Byng in Spring

"The girl is dead for sure, but I think this guy is still alive! Go get help!"

The Paramilitary Family

Although visual Face Time and the regular ring of my new cellular telephone emit different sound tones, I sometimes get confused. Consequently, I pulled the phone to my preferred ear only to hear, "Uncle R, you have a hairy ear."

It was my nephew, Ned. "Hi Ned," I switched the phone from my ear to face, "What's up, no school today?"

"Early dismissal day."

"What does that mean?" I asked, wiggling my nose and eyebrows.

"Who knows? The teachers have something to do and once a month they let us out early at two in the afternoon."

"That's nice," I said with a chuckle. "What you up to?"

"I need a responsible adult."

"Really, and you are calling me?" I said with a chuckle.

"Yeah, no duff eh, Mum nominated you. We are going to Camp Byng on the Sunshine Coast. And I need an accompanying parent and/or a responsible adult."

"Is this the *royal* we or anyone more specifically identifiable?" I asked.

"The Kitsilano Cub Scouts Spring Camp Out."

My sister Annette has two kids: Amelia, age fourteen, and Ned, at age eleven (and a-half by his count). My sister Annette was a handful as a child and it was reasonable to expect her children would be, too. However, such is not the case—they are all different. Personality is funny that way. Our dad often said, "See, every finger on my hand is different, same thing with my kids." The nature—nurture theoretical conundrum and family life gets complicated. It's hard to explain.

Ned and I have a good relationship. We do events whenever we can. Ned's life often gets busy with school and extra-curriculum schedules. Ned's biological father, Thomas, plays guitar in a blues band called *The Mahjeeroms.* Although Thomas has been long gone for way longer than he was ever around, he pops by every now and then to show his side of the family flag. Thomas has always been kind to me and I reciprocate accordingly. Thomas and my sister had a difficult divorce. At the time neither had much money and that made the divorce process even more strenuous. However, Thomas became a minor music celebrity in some circles and Annette became a senior partner in a large law firm. Success is measured in relative terms. Sometimes money matters more than what we would wish to think.

Thomas keeps a pied-á-terre in Vancouver's Gastown. When nephew Ned was younger I often served as a conciliating go-between, picking him up and so on, so-forth. To this day my sister and Thomas have trouble speaking to one another. I do what I can, managing a Swiss disposition between them.

"So, Uncle R, what's the word, you in or what?"

"For sure Ned," I smiled, "I'm in."

Last winter Ned's Cub Scout pack, along with others from all over British Columbia, held their annual Science World Scouting Sleepover. The signup sheet read: One Hundred and Ten Years of Scouting. It was a big event and we could not miss it! Certainly, advertising the event as a "sleepover" was an oxymoron in the first degree. A "*wake over*" was more like it. They chattered amongst themselves all night long. The sounds of squirrels chattering was unending despite requests from those who thought they held some level of control.

Each geographic scouting group got their own section of Science World to set up an indoor campsite. I asked what that meant and learned it was "Just throw your sleeping bag down in a corner, and that's your spot." Then we circulated through the maze of Science World learning stations. In our group, Ned was the first to fall a sleep and the last to wake. "Loud noise doesn't bother me, I'm used to it." Ned said with a smile. "My mum and sister both make lots of loud noise, all the time."

Ned's older sister, Amelia, has been documented and described as a "gifted" girl. She speaks four or five languages, plays a few instruments, and is way too wise for a fourteen-year-old adolescent. When I arrived to take Ned to the Science World sleepover Amelia, as usual, had many questions. "Uncle R where's your uniform?"

"Sorry?" Amelia will bait me if I am not careful.

"*Ned is in the paramilitary!*" Amelia declared too loudly.

"Am not!" Ned shrieked from the other end of the house.

"Are too!" Amelia yelled back. "Uniforms, badges, and salutes, which is the basic definition and premise of a paramilitary."

Annette roared into the room, "Enough Amelia, and I mean it!"

"Relax mum, its sociology," Amelia explained.

"Annoying and unnecessary," Annette pointed her finger. "It stops now."

I gave Annette the thumb-up signal. "Hi sis, how you doing?"

She smiled, "As you can hear we are par for the course."

At that point Ned came slowly strolling into the room dragging his oversized backpack, sleeping bag, and rolled-up foam sleeping mattress. "Mum, did you ask him?"

"He just got here Ned. We have not had time to discuss it yet." Annette pleaded.

"Discuss what?" I asked.

"You ask him," Ned said looking at his mother.

I looked from one to the other and finally Annette said, "Ned wants to bring Georgie to the sleepover. He doesn't want him to be lonely at home here without Ned."

"Okay, who is Georgie?" I innocently asked.

"*Georgie is a stuffed monkey*," Amelia yelled from her room down the hall. "My baby brother cannot sleep without his cuddle monkey."

Annette stormed off to deal with Amelia. "Let's get out of here Ned." I said grabbing his backpack. "Put Georgie in here. We're cool, pitter patter let's get at her." On that note we loaded the car and took off for the Kitsilano Cub Scouts Spring Campout at Camp Byng on the Sunshine Coast. Ned is a great kid. He is eleven and in Piagetian psychological terms he is still developing, maturing and growing. He wasn't leaving Georgie behind—he'd be lonely.

Ned ~
We Can't Colour Worth Crap

Shane Bighill has always been extremely weird. Everybody knows that is true. He is weird and that is a fact. When we were in the fourth grade Shane was an ace foursquare player, king's corner, handball, or whatever you want to call the game. Shane was good. Nobody could ever best him, but Shane had a thing about stepping on cracks. Logan said it's early onset OCD.

"OCD?" I asked.

"Ned, obsessive compulsive disorder!" Logan said with authority.

Logan makes like he knows these things, but I wonder. He doesn't know everything even though he always makes like he does. We were on our way to Camp Byng. My Uncle R and I had arrived at the Horseshoe Bay rendezvous point where we were all going to take the forty-minute ferry ride together. Shane, Logan, Raj and I were a camping foursome.

You can count on Logan being early and Shane is *always* late. And it does not mean anything to me; it's just the way they are. But, not Logan, he always takes a shot at Shane. When Raj's mother dropped Raj and Shane off at the ferry terminal's appointed meeting spot, Logan just had to lob, "Shit Shane, you are always late." Logan liked pushing Shane's buttons.

"Piss off Logan," Shane shot back, "You white people are always stuck on time."

Raj Gill rounded out our foursome. He is always even keeled, but joined in the gupshup with, "Sorry Shane, look in a mirror, *you* are white! You have *red* hair."

"So what!" Shane gets agitated easily. "I am Black Irish!"

I was determined to stay out of this discussion. It goes nowhere and I have already heard it, way too many times, Shane's Black Irish story. He says his grandfather is a Blackfoot First Nations Indian and his grandmother is second generation Irish-Canadian, but his great grandfather is *Black Irish* from Donegal.

When I asked my Uncle R, he explains that the Black Irish term is a bit *generic* and ambiguous, but there is an old history and some say it is true. The theory suggests descendants from the Spanish Armada are the Black Irish. While others say the Black Irish are Irish African descendants migrated from the British Caribbean region. Uncle R says, "People mingle, mix, and marry, and it improves the gene pool."

"Shane, you are always late." Logan can't let anything slide.

"My grandfather is from the Punjab," Raj explained. "He is always on Punjabi time."

"What does that mean?" Logan asked.

"It means things get done when they get done. Don't sweat the small shit Shane."

"I'm not sweating anything," Shane said, "Logan and the white people, that's what I'm talking about."

"Shane, you are *white*!" Logan always pushes his buttons. "You have red hair."

And that was that. This always ends the same way with them brawling, but making like nobody is going to get hurt, until somebody gets hurt. And you know that somebody *always* gets hurt.

Scouter Jess is one of the nicest leaders in our troop. She and my Uncle R came scrambling over to separate the goofballs and move us over to the ferry lineup. All the formal leaders are called Scouter *this* or Scouter *that.* There are a lot of old traditions in traditional Scouting, but there are changes, too. Not that I would know because I only know how things are now. Evidently, in the past there were no girls in Scouting. I didn't know that because we have lots of girls in our group. We've got Sheila, Jenny, Nicole, Johanna, Emily, Janice, and some other girls whose names I always forget. We got girls; maybe we got too many girls, if you ask me. Uncle R says it's something I'll get over some day. What do I know anyway, I'm only eleven years old, but as mum says, "Getting older everyday."

We all go to Kitsilano Elementary School and this year the sixth grade is easier for most of us, except Shane. Uncle R explains, "Once Shane discovers he does not have to be so defensive a lot of everyday life will become easier." Scouter Jess says, "You can lead a horse to water, but you can't make her drink."

Certainly, Shane is not a purebred horse, but he is for sure a thoroughbred something, and he is just so high-strung, too. His twin sister Nina is the *opposite.* She has jet-black hair, she is easygoing, and never hassles anyone. Nina hardly never hangs out with us.

Fraternal twins are different than identical twins. Nina and Shane Bighill are the ying and yang of twins. Its not that one is evil and the other is nice, they are just opposites. My sister, Amelia, is three years older than me and we are very different, too. Amelia thinks she is too cool for school. "Get an online education, get home schooled," that's what I say. Amelia is peculiar, but Shane is worse, way worse.

We all hauled our camping gear to the ferry lineup. We're always lining up for something. "Don't colour outside the lines."

Uncle R and I are both left-handed—can't colour worth crap.

Raj Gill ~
Boys are a Blessing

Logan Meyers keeps saying our friend Shane Bighill shows mental crazy behaviours. Ned Reilly tells him to just cool it because Logan does not know what he is talking about. "Shut up, Logan, Shane is okay, just leave him alone. Quit pushing his buttons. You only do it for your entertainment." Ned pointed his index finger at Logan and sneered in disgust.

I know that part is true because whenever Logan is bored during recess break at school he does things that push Shane's buttons just to get him to spaz out. And you know Shane always spazs out, but it isn't really all that entertaining. Logan likes it.

Sometimes I think maybe I might be mental. "I often walk down the road talking out loud to myself all the time." I explained, "Practice, rehearsal, whatever you want to call it, I do it all the time."

"Raj," Ned scoffed, "don't sweat the small stuff. You are not mental."

"Thanks Ned," I smiled.

"Raj, we're cool," Ned fist pumped me with a big grin.

Along with all the other Cub Scout groups, we were on the giant ferryboat that was taking us across the ocean to Camp Byng for the Kitsilano Cub Scouts Spring Camp Out. It was great; after the

Scouter leaders got us to stash our gear at the front of the boat. And after they gave us a bunch more instructions, rules and reminders, we were free to run around the boat. "It's a boat," Ned said, "no one is going to get lost. Lets go get cheeseburgers!"

The burger and French fries lineup was quite long. It would take forever to get through to the cashier. We were at the wrong end of the line wondering what to do when Ned said, "Follow me, I have an idea."

Ned is good that way; he always knows what to do. While we were milling about the ferry terminal, and although the Scouter leaders told us to stay in our zone, Ned wandered over to the West Van zone. We followed Ned's lead. Ned makes friends easy. He had been joking around with the West Van group and they became fast friends. Sure enough it paid off in the burger line because one of the West Van Cub Scouts had a good spot up front in the line. Ned gave him our cash and he got us the burgers. It was great.

I was having a tonne of fun. I'd been looking forward to the boat ride. I'm the only member of my family that was born in Vancouver. Everyone else was born in the Punjab. Anyway, I'd never been on a big ferryboat before. I've been to India, twice, but this was my first ferry ride. I was only two years old the first time we went to India so I don't remember anything. We went again last year and it was weird. My sister, Parminder, says the relatives make such a fuss about me because "Everyone knows, boys are a blessing!"

"Buzz off, it's not my fault, Parminder," I clarified, "I didn't ask for any special treatment. I didn't ask for anything. It's the Indian way, what can I do about it?"

"Boys are a blessing." Parminder put her hands together, "Namaste."

We gulped back the burgers and went to the top deck of the ferry. The sun was shining, the wind was brisk, and we ran around like idiots. A tonne of fun and we were just getting started. We were going camping for the weekend. No sisters, parents, teachers, or city stuff, it's the Kitsilano Cub Scouts Spring Camp Out.

Logan Meyers ~ Second Born Stuff

I hate my parents, and I tell them so everyday. My mum's a lowercase Catholic and my dad is a Jew: I got the worst of both religious worlds. They are both too competitive. Both try to compete too hard to be strict with me. All those stupid rules are too much to handle. I hate it.

When I was five years old, my brother Ben died in a bicycle accident. My parents have never been the same since. First born stuff I guess. Benji was five years older than me, which made him ten when it happened. As I said, I was only five when it happened. What do five year olds know? Not much.

Benji and Daryl Reynolds were riding their bikes down the Arbutus Street hill. It is a steep hill. Lower Point Grey Road and the Arbutus Street intersection have cars, lots of cars. Upper Point Grey Road, where the rich people live, has no cars. The road is blocked except for bikes. Those boneheads shoulda been riding where the rich people live. Both boys flew through the intersection. Daryl made it and Ben did not. He got clipped by a car and sailed through the air landing on his back. Benji had the best helmet money could buy (my dad does that stuff), but it did not help much.

Benji did not die right away. It took a few days because they had him on "life support systems" and some sort of a breathing machine. My parents took me to the hospital to "visit" Ben before they "pulled the plug" to let him go. Guess it was another one of my parents' dumb ideas because I had a bad reaction at the hospital. I was five, what do you expect? I did some screams, called some names and generally had a bad reaction seeing Benji in the hospital. I had never heard of organ donations. I did not know what that meant—I was five years old.

The funeral was a big deal, but I did not have to go because my friend Ned Reilly's uncle came over to talk with my parents. Uncle R told them it would likely be a bit too traumatic for me to do the funeral thing. What's an open casket anyway?

For a few weeks after the funeral my parents and I had to visit a shrink for "family therapy." I took pills, and both my parents took pills the shrink prescribed. Ned's Uncle R is a shrink but a different kind. Uncle R does talk therapy no pills.

I like Ned's Uncle R. We all call him Uncle R now. Unofficially he is an uncle to our little group of goofballs. Last year Uncle R went with us to the Cub Scouts Science World Sleepover. While we were there stupid Shane Bighill could not calm down and go to sleep when we were told it was lights out time. So Uncle R took Shane for a walk in the rain. Talk therapy worked for Shane. He came back, unzipped his sleeping bag, and went to sleep.

I don't hate my parents because Ben died. It was not their fault. It was an accident. I hate all their rules, supervision, and constant craziness. Let me breathe. I'm just an eleven-year-old kid. I am one year older than when Ben died. Lets celebrate. I'm already on borrowed time.

After Ben's accident I saw a lady shrink for a few weeks, but while I was there all I did was play with a sandbox, draw pictures and eat gummy bears. There was nothing wrong with me. Benji died, okay, it happened, I'm over it. The lady shrink and my parents agreed that 'monitoring' would be the way forward for me.

Here we are six years later with full on monitoring, no end in sight. I hate it.

My mum still sees a shrink. She's got a bunch of bottles of pills in her bathroom. And I have been told, repeatedly, in no uncertain terms, "Stay out of mum's bathroom and don't touch stuff!"

My mum is a musician. She is a violin player, and everyone knows music people are weird, eh. She has some violins that I can touch, but there is a red one that is "priceless" and no one touches the red one. Violins are loud.

Ned Reilly's real dad is a musician, but unlike my mum Ned's dad is nowhere near classical music. Ned doesn't see his real dad very often, but he's cool with it. Besides he has his Uncle R.

The day before the Cub Scout Camp Byng thing my parents weirded out on me about the camp consent form. Originally, my dad was going to accompany me and the form was not needed. Now he is saying he can't go because of "business" and we need to talk about the "camping thing." My dad is a stockbroker. There is no business on Saturdays. The markets are closed and he just does not want to go camping in the woods. I knew this would happen!

My mum tried to help and pretend to understand, but it only accelerated my dad's excuses and my anger. "I'm eleven years old! I'm not a baby! No one will die, just sign the freaking form and let me go camping!" I know yelling does not help, but I do it anyway. What else could I do?

"Logan, it is not that simple," my mum said. "There are issues."

"No there aren't any issues!" I screamed. "Just because dad does not want to go that should not mean I cannot go."

My dad blathered on about my lack of understanding, grabbed his car keys, and took off in a huff. You know that always helps the discussion.

My mum telephoned the group leader, Scouter Bob Pritchard. I only heard her end of the conversation, but whatever he said I guess it was good enough to get her to sign the consent form and let me go camping.

"Mr. Pritchard says Ned Reilly's uncle will be staying with your group. I think that is nice, Logan. He is a nice man." She handed me the form. "I hope you have fun camping."

"You know I hate you, right?"

She started crying, "I wish you wouldn't say such things, Logan."

"Too bad."

Annette Reilly
is Really Stressed Out

These days it seems that I am stressed out all the time. *Working in the law* firm, single mum raising two kids, and dealing with daily difficulties stresses me out beyond the threshold of coping and hoping. And then my big brother Randal comes over to try and set me straight.

"Sis, you've got it made in the shade. Your first world problems don't add up to much in relative terms, lighten up, and take a breath. You're okay."

"Oh sure, easy for you to say," I knew his logic had merit, but didn't want to give in too easily. "I don't know Randal, sometimes it all seems too much."

"Sis, here's some free therapy," Randal held up his hand palm toward me. "Stop it."

"Would if I could." These discussions with my bro always take me back to childhood antecedents. "Amelia is a lot to handle."

"What?" Randal made a scowling face, "she's a gift."

"Yes, the school psychologist tested her, and says she is gifted." I shook my head. "IQ off the Richter scale."

"There you go," Randal smiled, "it's a documented empirical gift."

"Nowadays Amelia talks nonstop about epistemology."

"That is so cool." He gave me a thumb up signal.

"Not really. Last week's discussions centered around contract law and specifically, the social contract. I'm a lawyer and I can handle those discussions. This week it is the science of science orations that are putting me under."

"Ned eats dirt." Randal pointed at me.

"He does not! It is the five second food on the ground rule deployment." My son Ned is a boys' boy. Life is easy with him, and for him. He sleeps soundly. Amelia is awake all the time. "People always show sympathy for the mums with autistic kids, Downs syndrome, whatever, but not the mums with a gifted kid."

"Annette, two words," now he held up his both palms, "*Stop it!*"

Amelia Might Fly

Ned says he doesn't remember ever living with both of our parents at the same time, but I do. We lived in the little yellow house and my bedroom had green walls. Ned's bedroom walls were blue because my parents knew he was going to be a boy before he was born.

I was named after Amelia Earhart who was a woman aviator. She died trying to circumnavigate the world. Amelia Earhart disappeared somewhere in the central Pacific Ocean. To this date neither her body nor airplane has ever been found.

Linguistically speaking, Ned's name is a rebracketing of Eddard or Edmund. My mum says Ned was *not* named after Eddard Stark in the Game of Thrones, but I know he was because our father favoured the series. And they were under pressure to produce a name. They had too much time to debate boys' names before he was born. In the end Ned was something they could both agree on.

Father is a musician and my mum is a lawyer. Of course they were not likely to succeed or sustain any level of compatibility. Birds of a feather flock together. Father is a Meadow Lark and mum's a Goshawk. Fine by me. Genetically I did well between the two of them. A paternal music gene and my mum's language proclivity serve me well. On my fifth birthday my father presented me with a starter Gibson guitar. Never one to be outdone my mum gave me a computer-based

French language programme with hierarchical software. I did French and German the first year. It's Rosetta.

Currently I am working over both parents, singularly and concurrently, for a new stand-up string bass violin as well as the acquisition of some language nanobots. Both parents always start from a position of negative and I always have to pull them to the positive side. It is never easy.

Father is a musician and acquiesces on my need for new instruments; he hesitates on lessons, and worries about storage conditions. I know he'll come through for me.

My mum makes like she's the master of practicality. She likes logic. Einstein freely admitted that there were lots of things that he could not understand. And it was not a problem for him. My mum tries to understand everything.

"Mum, you don't understand how your car works, but you drive everyday," I explained politely.

"Amelia, that is not true," Mum was defensive. "I took auto-shop in High School! I understand how cars work."

"Okay, good thing cars have not changed much in the twenty years since you graduated," I said dismissively. "You use the microwave oven everyday. I bet you do not know how it works?"

"Is there a point going to be made soon?" she asked.

"Yes, language nanobots are like your microwave," I pleaded. "You do not need to understand everything about them to use them!"

"But, if I am buying them, I want to know *something* about them."

"I am struggling with comprehension syntheses of some of the Asian languages. There was a guy on the intraweb who put me onto the bots to help translate and learn complex languages."

Sometimes my mum tilts her head with a neurological intent on understanding from a different angle. "Is this the same teacher that convinced me you need a special computer to process mathematical algorithms?"

"Mum, no," I shook my head, "that was math and this is language. Remember, when your Apple computer burnt out because I needed a co-processer to handle the structural equation modeling algorithms?"

Currently, I am enrolled in an online school for exceptional students. "That math class is over and I am onto new stuff now."

The online school uses the traditional Internet and a dedicated Intraweb to deliver instructional portal packages. Once a week we meet with the instructors at a brick and mortar satellite school downtown. It's okay, and not as boring as the regular school.

Mathematics meant a lot to me for a while. I liked binary components, elements, and equations. Right or wrong was attractive. Balanced equations and models made sense. Things add up, or they can be subtracted, multiplied or divided. Once I got heavily immersed in higher-level algebra the elements became more philosophical and abstract. I liked concrete math. My mum won't talk to me about epistemology. I think she's frustrated.

My mum taught me how to read when I was three years old. It was a bigger deal for her than me. Uncle R started the whole thing with a reading acquisition method called "neurological imprints." It was sorta like Konrad Lorenz's canine imprint training, but with kids not dogs. But, when my mum got overzealous about the whole thing, Uncle R said, "Amelia is just barking at the words. Comprehension and applications are higher levels compared to basic word decoding."

We started with picture books that had prose on the bottom. My mum would read a few lines and then say, "your turn." I could guess what was next or had heard the book a few times and could remember the text. Like playing piano "by ear."

By the time I was five we were reading Judy Blume and Roald Dahl novels. Uncle R still stuck to the idea that I was basically barking at words without understanding what I was actually *reading*. My mum agreed. It took her a while, but she agreed. "Amelia needs to mature on a natural time-line, not yours Annette." Uncle R explained to my mum. "Don't push her."

Reading comprehension is more important than decoding. My mum understood and backed off enough to let me breath freely, for a while. Don't be a helicopter mum.

For a while she thought I needed more social situations. Mum thought I should get out and be more gregarious. She put Ned into a paramilitary organization. Ned is the most gregarious person I know. Everybody loves Ned. He joined the Cub Scouts, got a uniform, slogans and salutes. I was too old and definitely did not want to join anyway. "Mum, I am alone, but I am not lonely."

I would like to take flying lessons. How old do you have to be to get a pilot's license?

Who is Normal?

"Uncle R," nephew Ned called from the other side of the ferry's cafeteria table, "now that we have finished eating, okay if we go outside to look for whales?"

I smiled, knowing the likelihood of seeing whales at this time of year was low, and really all they wanted to do was run around, mingle, whoop and holler. "Of course," I answered, "but Ned, remember when they make the announcement saying we are nearing the terminal, make sure everyone shows up on time at our area to pickup their gear."

Logan Meyers salutes and answers for Ned, "You got it Uncle R!"

"Logan, no need to salute," I responded.

Shane Bighill cannot be outdone by Logan. He salutes and repeats, "You got it Uncle R."

I just smiled and faux waved as they rushed on out the door to the outer decks. It's only a forty-five minute ferry ride from Vancouver to the Sunshine Coast. We dock at Gibson's Landing where charter buses are waiting to take us to Camp Byng, which is about ten minutes north near Roberts Creek. The time travels too quickly when you are young.

The sun was shining, but the wind was brisk when I walked outside and up the stairs to the top deck. Cub Scouts from all parts of the province were on the ferry. Some similar uniforms, but different hats, neck scarves, woggles, and distinguishing markings set the different groups apart. The Kitsilano group was easy to locate because Shane Bighill and Logan Meyers were up to their usual shenanigans. With the voice of a foghorn Shane was telling Logan where to go and how to get there. I was on my way over to separate the scufflers, but Scouter Kimberly got there first. Of course, I capitulated to Scouter Kim, she outranks me. That is, considering I hold no rank in this organization. Scouter Kimberly, on the other hand, ranks high.

"Break it up you two," Scouter Kimberly commands. Although she is not that big herself, Scouter Kim can appear larger than she looks and the boys do not want to test her patience.

"He started it," Shane said, spitting while speaking.

"Don't care," Scouter Kim said with a stern tone. "I do not want to see that kind of behaviour from Cub Scouts, in uniform, in a public place!"

"It's not my fault," Shane pleaded. "Logan called me OCD mental."

Scouter Kimberly was not abetting, "Don't care Shane," she raised her palm. "Remember, sticks and stones may break my bones but words will never hurt me."

"Logan's bullying me." Shane knew the buzzwords to use.

"He's lying," Logan chimed in. "All I did was laugh at him because Shane is funny."

"Enough already!" Kim was not interested in antecedents. "We are close to docking soon. Let's go get our gear and get ready to leave."

Although I am off the clock, and on a theoretical holiday, I can't help but diagnose Shane's situation as dysemia. He has trouble reading between the lines. He cannot read a person's facial expression and see the difference between anger, sadness or happiness. It is a type of nonverbal learning disability. Shane is a smart kid. I have seen him in various situations where he shows a high level of cognitive functioning, but it some social settings he hasn't a clue.

The diagnostic criteria and their implications are unsettling in many circumstances. Who decides these things? Concede to consensus.

Dysgraphia (writing problems), Dyslexia (reading), Dyscalculia (mathematics), Dyspraxia (developmental coordination disorder) and all the other "dysfunctions" which suggest someone has an abnormality. Who is normal?

My father is still working as an anthropologist at the University of Winnipeg. He is so proud that he and his colleagues took the administration to court over mandatory retirement and they won. "I'm not officially old yet Randy," (dad is one of the very few who still call me Randy).

Dad is a big Albert Einstein fan. In his Princeton office, Einstein had a sign saying: Not everything that counts can be counted, and not everything that is counted counts.

Dad and Annette could argue for hours on about almost everything and anything. It was their thing. They still do it whenever they get together. Old habits die hard.

When my office mate, Harjit, and I had our big York Avenue Psychology Practice office-opening gala, dad drove in from Winnipeg. For my office, he had commissioned a cartoon caricature showing a person sitting alone in an auditorium under a big banner that read: Conference for Normal People.

"Thanks dad, this is my office Einstein sign."

I was shaken from my daydream when Ned came running up to me, tugging on my sleeve, saying, "C'mon Uncle R, the ferry is docking soon. We have to muster and get our gear."

Kaw Kah Caw

"Oh, Ned," my mother reads and recites research while I eat breakfast. "Says here, Camp Byng," she swivels her screen, "is one of a number of campsites owned and operated by Scouts British Columbia, but Byng is the biggest with over two hundred and eight acres."

"That's nice," I said with a nod, "please pass the jelly."

Undeterred she turned the screen back to face her and continued, "Wow, Camp Byng has twelve hundred metres of ocean foreshore." Shaking her head with a smile, "Your grandpa, the anthropologist, would say a mile of waterfront. He won't go metric."

"Why not?"

"Oh, he's old, and doesn't need to change."

"Cool enough."

Pointing back to her screen with more excitement, "Now here's what Head Scouter Ron mentioned. Camp Byng has four main lodges with a number of sleeping hulls."

"Okay."

"Yes, so you are sleeping in a hull with Logan, Shane, Raj, Uncle Randal, and an Eagle Scout. It is a check and balance system Scouts Canada developed."

"What's that?" I asked without much of a clue what she was on about.

"Children cannot sleep in tents or dorms with only one adult. There must be at least two adults present."

"Got it." My mum is a belt and suspenders lawyer. She leaves nothing to chance. No worries: Her trousers will never fall down. Every t is crossed and every "i" is dotted. Two adults sleeping with children means nothing bad can happen without a witness. Mum's big on witnesses. I did not want to spoil her mood by asking what if both adults were bad or untrustworthy. Didn't matter anyway because my sister Amelia came into the room.

"What are you two on about?" she asked.

"We're just looking at the history of Camp Byng."

"What's the thing with Byng?" Amelia asked, pretending she cared.

"You remember," mum's index finger went straight up, "I told you Ned was going camping today with Uncle Randal and the Kitsilano Cub Scouts."

Nodding her head, "Right, okay, did Uncle R join the paramilitary too?"

"If you please, there's no need, Amelia," Mum knew her routine.

"What?" Amelia pretending dismay, "just asking."

I took that as my cue to get up and leave the breakfast table. "Gonna go finish packing."

Mum corrects, "Yes, good idea, you are *going* to finish packing. Uncle Randal will be here soon."

Uncle R is my mum's brother. She says he is eccentric. He says she is paralyzed by perfectionism. They are both a bit right and both a bit too critical. I like Uncle R. He's nice to me. Maybe he is eccentric, but he's nice to me.

When Shane Bighill gets older they'll probably say he's eccentric. Right now he's just an eleven-year-old kid and he gets all kinds of labels, but eccentric isn't one of them.

I hate packing. My mum would do it for me, but then my sister says she is encouraging my learned helplessness. I pack my own stuff. I hate packing. We're only going for two nights, back on Sunday, why do I have to pack anything?

From the other end of the house I could hear that Uncle R had arrived. Amelia has to ask him where is his uniform? Why is he wearing civilian clothes? And then, just to bug me she has to say, "Ned is in the *paramilitary!*" She says that because Cub Scouts wear uniforms, salute and stuff.

Of course, I yell back to her that "*Am not!*" And that in turn sets off my mum who spaz attacks Amelia's attitude. They always carry on too long.

I dragged my stuff down the hall and Uncle R suggested we should bail out of here. "Good idea, let's go!"

As I said, Uncle R is eccentric. He is a car-guy. But having said that he also has a motorcycle (mum calls it a donor cycle because she thinks it is dangerous) and a pickup truck that he uses weekends on Mayne Island.

Last year, mum had a big trial, and it went on too long. She could not get out of court so she sent a text message to Uncle R asking him to pick me up after baseball practice. He showed up on his motorcycle. It was just great! I wore my baseball-batting helmet, sat in front of him, and held on to what is called a motorcycle gastank storage bag. The sun was shining bright, bees were buzzing, the birds were singing and I was having the time of my life. We were whooping and hollering while riding the motorcycle from the UBC Baseball Diamonds to our house in Kitsilano. We took the long way home.

For sure, I didn't tell her, and I doubt Uncle R told her, but mum found out about the motorcycle ride. She went *crazy*, I mean big-time crazy. I was in my room and could hear her on the telephone giving it to Uncle R with both barrels, reloading with machinegun fire. Why was she so angry? I had fun. A tonne of fun!

"Randal, you have done some stupid things in your life, but this is unconscionable. What were you thinking?"

I know it is hard to get a word in edgewise when mum is fired up. Uncle R probably tried to no avail. I'm sure he said sorry several times.

"What you did is not only illegal as *hell*, but just downright dangerous. Just think about it!"

Can't wait until I am sixteen. Uncle R says it will be perfectly legal for us to ride together on the motorcycle. At sixteen I can go to motorcycle school and get a license to ride. Mum will likely kibosh the idea, but I like to dream.

Today, as I suspected, because it is June and the weather is nice Uncle R's little red two seater Austin Healey Bug Eye Sprite convertible was parked out front. He loves that car. Mum hates it, thinking it is only marginally safer than the motorcycle. It is street legal, four wheels, and old.

One of Uncle R's patients gave him the car. There was a big to-doo about the car because psychologists are not allowed to accept gifts from patients. My mum had a legal opinion, Uncle R's wife, Harjit, had an opinion (and she is an Appeals Court Judge) and the guy's wife had an opinion, too. The owner died and left the car to Uncle R in his will. No big deal, keep the car, eh.

Uncle R and Harjit have been together for over twenty years or so, but my mum always emphasizes, "It's a common law marriage." Amelia says Aunty Harjit is a Sikh and they didn't have a traditional Christian church marriage. Mum has issues with too many things anyways, but mum makes like she doesn't. She does, and everybody but her knows it.

We loaded my gear in the car, fastened our seatbelts, and blasted off down the road heading to the Horseshoe Bay ferry terminal. Uncle R had been to the Mayne Island Farm Gate Store and had a big bag of my favourite Shanti McD's chocolate chip muffins. These muffins are the best ever. She uses some special chocolate or something. Pace and gluttony are always hard with these muffins. "You want one Uncle R?" I motioned to the bag, but he smiled and shook his head. "No thanks, Ned. They're all yours."

At first the traffic was not too bad, but after all it is a two-bridge sojourn, which means anything can happen. Uncle R drives fast. My mum is a dawdler. She drives slow and conservative. Uncle R says he is assertive not aggressive. We flew over the Burrard Street Bridge, took a shortcut down Beach Avenue, and stalled out in a Denman Street traffic jam. Eventually we made it through Stanley Park, over the Lions Gate Bridge to the highway. The trip's balance was breezy and easy. We made it in relatively good time considering it was Friday afternoon.

Logan Meyers, who is always early for everything, was waiting at the rendezvous point. "Hi Ned," Logan waved. "Just put your gear over here. We are starting a pile."

"Who put you in charge?" I asked.

"I'm not in charge," Logan scoffed, "just following the leader, Scouter Ron's orders. He told me our group's stuff goes here."

"No worries Logan," I said with a smile. "Where's the rest of our group?"

"Ah, you know, Shane is always late. I don't know about Raj. I think they're carpooling together" Logan shrugged.

Almost on cue Shane and Raj pulled up in Mrs. Gill's minivan. They clambered out, began dragging over their gear when Logan and Shane started jawing each other with insults. They always do this dance. And it is always boring. It always ends the same way. Uncle R and Scouter Jess broke them apart and we loaded onto the ferry.

The ferry ride was a lot of fun. We ate cheeseburgers, fries, and ran around the ferry playing tag on the top deck. We mingled with other Cub Scouts from all over the place. Before you knew it we docked on the other side of the water where there were a dozen or so big yellow buses waiting to take us to Camp Byng. The buses travelled cavalcade, we sang songs and bumped along the road until we got there.

When we arrived, everyone piled out of the buses only to have to line-up again. Signs were posted showing us where to hoof it to our campsite. There are four main lodges at Camp Byng, each has a dormitory and lots of sleeping hulls scattered about the site. We found our assigned lodge and then quickly picked a sleeping hull.

Raj, Shane, Logan and I picked Hull Number 5. We dropped off our gear and began exploring. There were trails leading to the ocean and trails leading to the forest. All of a sudden three whistle tweets shrieked out for our attention. We all dropped everything and went running to the assembly station.

All our leaders were lined up together. "Right over here Cubs," Scouter Ron directed, "let's get in a formation." He pointed to a big fat man who was standing beside him. "I'd like to introduce Scouter Gary. He is the manager of Camp Byng and is here to explain how things work."

Scouter Gary stepped forward put his hands up over his head, started flapping, and loudly bellowed, "Kaw, Kah, Caw."

Of course, wouldn't you know it, my misfortune to be standing beside Shane Bighill. I like Shane, but he is just so weird, and these things set him off the Richter scale. With as equal decibel level, but with greater intensity and spitting, Shane shrieked back, "Kaw, Kah, Caw."

"Yes!" the fat guy seemed pleased for some reason or another. "What's your name Cub Scout?"

"Sir, Shane Bighill, sir!"

Logan was standing on the other side of me and elbowed me in the ribs with a muffled snort. Logan whispers in my ear, "Shane watches too much television. This isn't the army."

"Tell my sister," I whispered back.

Scouter Gary said, "Everybody, listen closely, this is *very* important." He pointed his index finger at us from one end to the other. "This is bear country. Camp Byng has many bears. This is June. Bears are hungry." Then he pointed at Shane, "Cub Scout Shane here is a smart kid. If you see a bear, and you just might see one while you are here, you do exactly as Shane did. Yell, Kaw, Kah, Caw, as loud as you can. Make yourself look bigger by putting arms over your head and wave them. You cannot outrun the bear, so don't try. Just keep yelling and slowly walk backwards. Hopefully the bear will walk away from you. Remember, most times the bear is scared of humans."

Scouter Ron nodded and took over saying, "And," he put his palm up in the air. "Remember the buddy system is the *rule* here. I mean it! Never ever go anywhere without a buddy. If you have to go to the bathroom in the middle of the night, go with a buddy."

Scouter Gary almost seemed to push Ron out of the way, "One more thing, no food in the sleeping hulls, nothing, no-thing, no food. Last week when the South Central Burnaby Cub Scouts were here they left pizza in their sleeping hull and sure enough a bear broke in to get the pizza. No food, please."

Next it was Scouter Kim to step forward with announcements, "Okay, buddy system, do not leave this campsite area, go have fun, and come running when you hear this dinner triangle ring!" She demonstrated the triangle ring, waved her wrist, and said, "Okay, go, but stay close by."

"Bingo-bango-daddy-oh, let's go! Raj, you're my buddy," I screamed and took off. "Trail to the woods!"

Raj was on my heels screaming some Punjabi chant, which made no sense to me, but I liked it. Bingo-bango is a song my bio-father wrote when I was a little kid. I like it and scream bingo-bango whenever I can. I theorize dad hears it. Amelia says it is the absolute dumbest thing she has ever heard. However, truth be told, lately, I've overheard Amelia bingo-banging someone on her intraweb audio feed.

Although Logan and Shane spar at every opportunity they can, they are actually good buddies. Guess birds of a feather flock together.

They are both weird and that is their bonding friendship, I could hear them closing in on us. "Raj, this way," I said with a soft voice, "let's trick 'em." We took a sharp right turn and hid behind some shrubs. Sure enough not even ninety seconds passed when they came crashing along taking the bait.

"How long do you think it'll take until they figure it out?" Raj asked.

Snorting down a chuckle I whispered, "Let's give them a couple of minutes lead and then sneak up behind them. Well scare the shit out of Shane."

Raj smiled, gave me a thumb up sign. We brushed off the dirt and debris from our trousers and walked back to the trail. All of a sudden we hear Shane screaming "*KAW-KAH-CAW.*" From the tone we knew he wasn't goofing with us and then both Logan and Shane in unison shriek: "KAW-KAH-CAW, Ned, Raj, KAW-KAH-CAW!"

I looked over at Raj and he asked, "Bear?"

"Dunno," I shook my head, "but we gotta go help 'em!"

"Help them with a bear?" Raj asked.

"Dunno." I did not know what to say. "Let's go!"

We ran down the trail as fast as we could. Raj stumbled and did a face plant. I kept going. "Shane, Logan," I yelled, "we're coming!"

The path opened up into a clearing. I could see a young woman hanging from a tree. Next to her Shane and Logan were bent over trying to talk to a man on the ground. Shane was frantic.

"Ned, she's dead, but I think this guy is still alive," Shane bellowed at me.

Logan pointed to the broken branch and the rope around the guy's neck, "I think they were trying to hang together, you know, at the same time, but this guy's branch broke. His skin's not cold like her. Think he's still alive."

By this time Raj had arrived. "Ned, you know First-Aid, right?"

"Yes, I do," I said loosening the weird fabric-type rope off from the guy's neck. "Logan, listen close, go get my Uncle R or any leader. Them tell to call for emergency help!"

Shane bellowed, "What about me?"

"You go with Logan, get help!" I nodded my head to them.

Last year Uncle R and I took kayak lessons at the Jericho Beach Kayak Centre. They taught us the Inuit roll, paddling strokes and Cardiopulmonary Resuscitation. I thought it was boring, but paid enough attention to pass the test to get the piece of paper and badge so I could use the solo kayak rather than going in the double. Today was not a dress rehearsal, it was the real deal, and I got the CPR started.

"Raj," I ordered, "start timing me and watch what I'm doing, we're gonna have to take turns."

"Okay," he said, "what do you want me to do?"

I kept doing mouth-to-mouth resuscitation for a couple minutes and then said, "Okay Raj, you take over the mouth-to-mouth. I'm gonna pound on his heart."

Raj's eyes were larger than usual he looked like a deer-in-the-headlights, but he agreed, changed places with me and took over. I started doing the heart massage like we were taught. It seemed like Shane and Logan had been gone for an awfully long time, "Raj, how's the time going?"

He looked at his watch, "Five minutes, seventeen seconds."

Really, it seemed so much longer.

"When will the help get here?" Raj asked.

"Dunno," I kept doing the heart massage.

The time seemed to go so slow. Finally, Uncle R and Kim came thundering down the path. I could hear 'em before I could see them.

"Okay Ned," Uncle R tapped my shoulder. "Good work, I'll take a turn."

I moved out of the way, Uncle R and Kim took over.

"How long have you been here, Ned?" Kim asked. "How long have you been giving him CPR?"

"Ask Raj," I pointed, "he's been timing."

"Five minutes, thirty-four seconds," Raj responded.

Dr. R. –

Juvenile PTSD & Adolescent Angst

The birds were singing, bees buzzing, and Cub Scouts were staking turf, setting up sleeping hulls and running around Camp Byng. The quartet of boys that I was theoretically chaperoning had selected a sleeping hull, threw their gear inside, and took off *exploring.* Our designated zone had eight sleeping hulls to choose from. Basically the sleeping hull consisted of an elevated plywood floor, plywood walls with a blue tarpaulin tacked onto the roof's frame. It was basic shelter. A bit warmer than a tent, but not by much.

I had long lost sight of Ned, Raj, Shane and Logan. That happened faster than I expected. Their whereabouts worried me a little and I ambled over to chat with Scouter Kimberly Leonard to get a second, but informed opinion. She sort of seemed to say not to worry too much when I mentioned losing track of the boys. "They'll be back soon enough when the dinner triangle rings," Kim said with a smile. "They are working up an appetite."

Kim is pretty cool and collected. She works as an ER nurse at the UBC Hospital. Takes a lot to rattle Kim. In her work she has seen a lot of catastrophes with a range from simple to sublime. Definitely a good person to have on a camp out, experienced but laid back enough to know not to sweat the small stuff.

We were talking about the history of Kitsilano Cub Scouts when all of a sudden Shane and Logan came out of the wooded area screaming at the top of their lungs, "Help, Uncle R, somebody, we need help!" Shane was waving his arms, "Kaw, Kah, Caw!"

Logan was on his heels yelling, "We found a dead girl, but the guy is still alive. Ned's doing some sort of first aid stuff!"

We got up from our seats, ran towards them, "Whoa-whoa," I asked, "what's going on?"

They tried to talk and catch their breath at the same time. Kim said, "Take us to them, now!"

Kim called for emergency help, grabbed her walkie-talkie, nodded to me, "Let's go."

Shane and Logan pointed out the path and the direction, which was all we needed. It did not take long until we found Ned and Raj. Kim quickly checked the teenage girl who was hanging from the tree. She looked at me and shook her head.

I tapped Ned on the shoulder and said, "Okay Ned, good work, I'll take a turn."

Kim checked his pulse, pupils, and said, "He's alive, but barely. Let's hope we get some help soon."

"How long will that take?" I asked.

Kim just rolled her eyes and said, "Soon, real soon."

We did CPR, artificial respiration, heart massage thumps for what seemed like an eternity, but by Raj's timer it was only another five minutes. The first responders were firefighters. A guy named Norm seemed to push me out of the way and said to his partner, "Blaine, you bag him, I'll start the heart."

Two minutes later a helicopter dropped a stretcher basket to medevac the guy who still had some life in him. The coroner was summoned to attend to the girl.

By this time the crowd of Cub Scouts, leaders and bystanders had grown large and the situation needed to be defused, debriefed, and dealt with accordingly. Shane Bighill, rightfully so, was pretty manic and messed up. The other boys were busy chatting about what had happened.

Ron Weatherly, the head scout leader was doing crowd control and attempting to organize the group's return to the campsite. He softly spoke to Kim, "We need to start calling parents. We're done here."

Part Two

Consciousness –
Regaining & the Losses

Regaining consciousness was complicated. I slipped in and out so many times that it is hard now to know real from surreal. The look on Banny's face, that was different, it was real, and I will never forget it.

My mother crying, wailing, moaning, and hovering over me in the hospital room was unsettling, too. Having said that, the beginning was beauty and love, hospitals not so much. The hospital's smell was weird, pungently antiseptic, but barfy too.

Let me tell you about the beginning: I met Banerjee Malik at UBC. She was the most beautiful woman I had ever seen in my life. Her hair was raven's black, shiny and long. Her eyes almond coloured and a smile to light the room, she would tilt her head and nod with understanding at the important lecture points. We were in the same Organic Chemistry class together. She sat two rows in front of me and one seat to the left. I could see she took lots of notes, listened closely, and seemed to understand everything Professor Hirabayashi said and wrote on the white board screen. I did not understand hardly anything and whatever notes I did take made no sense, but oh, oh, oh, that Banerjee Malik was the most beautiful woman I had ever seen. I tried so hard not to stare.

Banny was eighteen and I nineteen. Some may have thought it coincidence, but I thought of it as a destiny omen when I discovered we both lived in the same dormitory, Totem Park. At first she tried to ignore me and pretend not to want anything to do with me. We walked together to and from class. At first Banny did not even want to walk with me, but her friend Jodie Giardini from my Sociology class vouched for me. "Harry is a good guy, Banny. He helped me with the stupid midterm exam. He's probably a pervert, but got me through the midterm."

I freaked out when Jodie uttered the pervert thing. The look on my face must have said something alarming. "Ah, I'm just joking, Harry is okay," Jodie playfully slugged me on the shoulder. Everybody laughed, but I was so nervous around Banny. She was so beautiful.

I thought the walk from chemistry class on Mackenzie Road to the Totem Park dorm on Marine Drive was too short and went too fast. I asked Banny to help me with organic chemistry because for sure I would fail if she did not help. I could not understand the chemistry concepts. We would study in the Totem Student Lounge area. Banny explained that I could not see the forest for the trees. "Harpreet," she often called me by my Sikh name, rather than Harry, my nickname. "It is just like a Tetris problem." Shaking her head she suggested, "Harpreet, just slow down, you need to fit the puzzle pieces together. It is really not that complicated."

All of a sudden, I got it. The loonie dropped. She was such good teacher and, very importantly noted, I *passed* the class. Banny and I became inseparable. We fell in love.

It was a wonderful time. That is, until the university term ended and it was time to go back home. We stayed on at Totem Park dormitory until the last of the students were ordered to vacate and go somewhere else. Reluctantly we returned to our respective family homes.

Banny's family has a big farm near Pitt Meadows, a suburb outside Vancouver. My family has a fabric and upholstery shop just off Main Street and 49th Avenue in Vancouver. Uncle has one in Surrey, but we are not competitive families.

It was terrible when we were separated by distance and family duties. It was hard not to see Banny everyday. It was worse to not talk to her, too. Her voice, the sound of it was something I missed most. Her touch was another thing. Oh, how I missed Banny.

I tried to telephone, but her cell phone no longer worked. I called her family landline telephone with no luck either. The person who answered simply said, "Banerjee is not available." Click.

Going crazy and not knowing what to do, finally out of the blue my cell phone rings, "Hello, Harpreet?"

"Banny," my heart was exploding. "Is that really you?"

"Yes, I am so, so, so sorry, my father took away my cell phone and I have not been able to call you until now. My mother watches me like a hawk. This is the first time I could get near a telephone."

"Why did your father take your cell phone?"

"He says the cell phone is *only* for family to call me and I am home now. No one needs to call me. I cannot argue with him. He is my father."

"Oh Banny, when can I see you?" I blurted. "I miss you more than I can say."

"I miss you, too." Banny made a sighing sound. "I love you Harpreet. Maybe next week."

"Next week," I moaned, "Banny, I can't wait that long!"

"I know, I know, but what can we do?" Banny softly sighed, "I have to go now," she whispered.

"No, no, not yet," I pleaded, but it was too late. The telephone was disconnected. I had to see her, but did not know what to do. She made it very clear that I could not show up at their farm. That would be a disaster; she said her father would freak out with an unknown uninvited young man wanting to see his daughter.

I waited and waited and waited to hear from Banny. I called her old cell phone a bajillion times hoping to hear her voice on voicemail. Nothing at all. It did not even ring anymore. I called the family farm landline with no luck, either. Banny never answered the landline and whoever did would not let me talk to her and they would not take a message, either.

Couldn't take it anymore, I had to see her. I took the bus, transferred three times and walked quite a ways to Banny's family farm. Wasn't what I expected, they had security. The only entrance in was through the front gate. They had cameras, intercoms, and a high fence. They would not let me in. I was not permitted to see Banny. I had no choice and went home feeling badly.

Rich people are so wacko. There are no caste customs in Canada!

Banny ~
Didn't Plan it This Way

My childhood was somewhat sheltered from the modern world, as most people know modern life, and my adolescence, forget it, that is another story altogether. Grandfather emigrated from the Punjab in the 1950s and began working in the outskirts of Vancouver in a Maillardville sawmill. Grandfather did well, socked away some solid money and bought a farm outside Pitt Meadows. The rest of the family moved in due course and the farm prospered. My parents had a traditional Indian arranged marriage and it was also correspondingly arranged that they would move to Canada to work on Grandfather's farm.

My father always said, "Banny, you are dumber than a doorknob," and my mother dutifully always said, "Banny, listen to your father."

Father was still angry that mother had born yet another daughter—me. Everyone knows, "Boys are a blessing." Mum went along with his traditions, but deep down, I guess she agreed.

Fortunately my grandparents were supportive and they helped me a lot! Great-grandmother worked as a nurse along side her husband who was a trained physician, but he always said she was the brains behind the operation. "She was way smarter than me with diagnostic skills beyond belief." He repeatedly told that to my paternal grandmother. When I said I wanted to be a physician she supported me, much to the distain of my parents. They did not dare contradict *their* elders. "Education is the key." Consequently, my path to medical school was charted, plotted, and after high school graduation I enrolled in the STEM Pre-Med Program at the University of British Columbia.

Although my parents were completely against the idea that I should think to live in the dormitory at UBC, they eventually conceded that the commute from the farm to the Point Grey UBC peninsula would take too much time out of the day. "Banerjee needs time to study," grandfather insisted. "The time it takes to travel to the city is a waste of time."

Grandfather came through for me and when I moved into the UBC Totem Park dormitory, freedom felt so wonderful that I began to cry. Of course I told my parents and grandparents that my tears were premature homesickness. My parents were sucked into the story, but grandmother winked her eye as they drove away. She knew and was happy for me.

I met Harpreet Dhaliwal in the Organic Chemistry class. I did not know what to think of him at first. He's such a city boy. I'm just a country bumpkin from the burbs. Harpreet seemed so worldly. He knew all the city stuff that I did not. He knew all the buses, skytrains, and seabus routes. We went to the top of Grouse Mountain. It took all day. We took the bus from UBC to the Seabus, travelled across the inlet and transferred to another bus to get to the Grouse Gondola. When we got to the top we could see for miles and miles. It was wonderful. Harpreet held my hand the whole way home.

Harpreet had trouble understanding some principles in chemistry, but he was a wizard with humanities. My friend Jodie said Harpreet helped get her through a confusing sociology course. Harpreet helped me understand university life in the big city.

Harpreet plays piano. One night he took me to the Orpheum Theatre to hear Keith Jarrett. It was mesmerizing. On the bus ride home Harpreet kissed me on the cheek. I was caught off guard and surprised, didn't know exactly what to do, so I kissed him back on his cheek.

Soon we were inseparable. Every day was so much fun. Harpreet could always make me laugh. He was silly, serious and insane with the things we would do. During the UBC Reading Break week we went to Whistler with a group from the dorm. Harpreet, he's such a good boy, certainly let his parents know his plans for Whistler. He tells them everything. I tell my parents nothing—I'm eighteen and out from their grasp. Nothing.

No way would I go downhill skiing, too dangerous. However, Harpreet taught me how to do skinny cross-country skiing on the Lost Lake tracked trails. A little scary in spots, but oh so pretty and lots of fun—I learned how to ski!

They had rented two condos side-by-side. Us four ladies were going to stay in one condo and the guys in the other. Another naiveté on my part when it was apparent sleeping arrangements evolved differently. The bedroom intended for Susan and I to share got occupied early. But it was okay, Harpreet and I slept on the foldout couch in the living room. Nothing untoward happened in the sense that we slept together with our clothes on. It was wonderful. Maybe Harpreet wanted to have sex, I don't know, because he did not pressure me for anything. We were happy to snuggle all through the night. And the morning's light came too soon. I woke with a smile inside Harpreet's arms holding me close.

Breakfast became a big event. "You can't go skiing on an empty tummy," Harpreet said with a smile as he mixed pancake batter. Everyone pitched in with the cooking and cleaning. After breakfast we went outside. It was cold, but invigorating. Diana and Ronnie went snowboarding at Blackcomb, Gayle and David went back to bed, Charmaine and Joey went shopping, while Harpreet and I went back to Lost Lake Passivhaus to rent skinny skis for cross county trails.

Whistler was the best time ever. I had so much fun. Like all good things it had to come to an end. I fell asleep on Harpreet's shoulder on the ride back to the dorm. Monday morning we were all back in our respective classes and Reading Break was over, but I still had a glow on and the memory lives forever.

The end of term loomed large on us. We spoke about it a couple of times, but only in passing. We did not want to deal with the issues. I had grown so accustomed to seeing Harpreet everyday that the thought of being apart did not seem normal. It didn't seem possible, yet it happened. We were getting evicted from the dorm. They put up signs in the elevator, slid a notice under the door, and then that was it, we had to leave. The academic term was over.

My parents came with a large pickup truck. I could tell father was in a mood. He was angry that I had so many boxes to be loaded into the truck. It almost seemed he would also prefer to not be bringing me home. Mother on the other hand made it clear: "There is a lot of work waiting for you back on the farm, Banny."

Woke up the next morning back in my old bedroom. At first I had forgotten where I was and thought I was still in the dorm until the loud farm noises brought me to my senses. I became fully awake when my mother burst through the bedroom door barking orders at me in Punjabi. I always answer in English, "You don't have to be so loud, mum. My hearing is good."

Undeterred, she got even louder, telling me to get up and get to work. "Okay, ok," I placated, as she pulled the covers off. I got up, washed, and went downstairs for breakfast.

First thing my father did when we got home last night was to demand my cell phone. I tried to keep it, but he got all hostile saying I did not need a cell phone now that I was back home. Reluctantly, I handed him the cell phone. I was a hostage in my home.

I knew Harpreet was trying to call. He even showed up at our front farm gate. It was no use, no one would let him in. I missed him terribly. One time when no one was looking I telephoned him from the pantry landline. It was wonderful to hear his voice.

The following week we were delivering seeds and feed to a farm near Powell River on the Sunshine Coast. I was allowed to go with the women for the trip. I telephoned Harpreet to tell him this news. He was so excited. "Banny, I cannot wait to see you!" He wailed on the other end of the line. "It has been too long since we have been together!"

"Yes, yes, I know what you mean. I cannot talk more. If I get caught talking on the telephone they will not let me go anywhere. I will meet you on the ferry boat." I could hear my mother's noisy shoes clomping down the hall and I could hear Harpreet continuing to say something about where on the boat, but I disconnected the telephone. He'd figure it out. It's a boat.

Finally, departure day arrived; we left the farm early in the morning and drove in heavy traffic to the ferry terminal. It seemed to take forever to get from the pay place to the inside of the ferry. They had us park down on the very bottom deck of the huge ferryboat. Everyone got out and started to make their way to the ferry's cafeteria. I said I wasn't hungry and asked if I could go to the top of the ferry to watch the water. Fortunately, nobody wanted to come with me. I climbed lots and lots of stairs until I finally got to the top and burst outside into the fresh sea air. It smelled briny and there was some wind blowing, but it was beautiful. I had to find Harpreet. First I went one way and then the other. My heart was beating hard and fast because of climbing all those stairs. Where was he? And then I saw him leaning on the railing, looking out at the sea. I started to walk quickly towards him.

Out of the corner of his eye he saw me, straightened up, and started screaming, "Banny, Banny, it is you!"

We had a heavy hug and I had to say, "Shush, shush, don't be so loud."

"I want to scream it to the world," Harpreet said so loud.

I kissed him hard on the lips to quiet him down. We were both crying tears of joy. "We cannot stay here," I whispered, "we have to go somewhere else."

"What do you mean?" Harpreet asked.

"I cannot have someone see me kissing you." I explained. "We won't need the trouble."

"Yes, yes, I understand," he smiled, "let's go sit in my mum's car."

I nodded and we skipped over to the down staircase. We went down a few flights of stairs, opened a sliding door and then we were in a sea of parked cars. We walked and weaved through the lanes, "Where is it?" I asked.

"Almost there," he pointed to the middle lane. "Ta-dah!" he grinned widely.

It was a white minivan with large red letters on the side: *Main Street Fabrics*. Underneath were Vancouver and Surrey telephone numbers. "That's not a car!" I exclaimed.

"I know," Harpreet waved his hands, "my mum thinks I am working, doing deliveries and pickups."

He beep-beeped the keys and the side sliding door opened automatically. We climbed into the back and sat with the rolls of fabrics. My heart was pounding so hard from all the skipping around and from seeing Harpreet again. I thought it would explode. Finally, I felt a little relaxed as he held me close and we listened to Keith Jarrett piano music.

Maybe I fell asleep or something, but all of a sudden someone was pounding on the side of the minivan, horns were honking and the ferry was unloading. "Oh shit," Harpreet shrieked, "the ferry is unloading!"

He seldom swears. Climbing up into the driver's seat, quickly starting the engine, and we were moving down the ramp. "Oh Harpreet, what shall I do?" I asked. "Everyone will be looking for me. I was supposed to meet them at the SUV truck before the ferry docked. I told them I would meet them before the ferry docked."

"Too late now," he said "we can catch them out on the highway, maybe."

"Maybe?" I asked.

"Yes, maybe," he looked over to me, "where are they going? Maybe we could meet them."

As we were driving off the ferry I could hear an announcement over the public address system: "Banerjee Malik, please report to the Chief Steward's office."

Harpreet tilted his head, gave it a shake, turned to me and said, "Too late now Banny, we are out of here." He stepped on the accelerator, changed lanes, and we surged forward fast.

"What should we do?" I asked. "Where are we going now?"

Harpreet, driving full speed ahead looked over to me. "You know what, I've been here before. When I was a kid my cub scout group came camping here."

"You were a Cub Scout?"

"Yes, yes, Lord Baden Powell, the whole thing, it's very Indian, you know."

I grinned, "Really."

"Yes, Rudyard Kipling and all those Rajs and galoots."

"Cub Scouts are from *England* not India." I declared.

"Maybe, dunno, but we were the 12th Central Vancouver Scout Group."

In my mind's eye picturing Harpreet in his cub scout uniform made me smile. It was so good to be back with him. We were driving down the road to a place called Camp Byng. He said it had been some years since he was last there, but he'd know it when he saw it. Fine by me because I felt free.

"That's it," he gave a thumbs up signal, "see the sign?"

"Yes, but we cannot go there," I scowled at Harpreet, "that is trespassing."

"No problem, we're cool, I now know exactly where we are and where we are going."

"Really?" I asked with a smile and a small poke to his ribs.

"Hey, hey, hey," he said trying to poke me back. "Of course, we are not going through the main gate, that *would* be trespassing. We are taking the back side road swinging behind the property's main zone to neutral turf. When we were kids the older scouts took us with them to this spot. It is where they smoked cigarettes."

"That is disgusting."

"What?"

"Smoking cigarettes."

"I never smoked! I'm a Sikh, just went with them because it was a cool pretty place to be."

"Peer pressure, eh?"

Harpreet just gave me one of his ear-to-ear smirks and we pulled into a little gravel parking lot.

"We've got to walk the rest of the way."

"Okay, *you* are the fearless leader," I said giving him the thumbs up signal back. Then we walked a kilometer or so until we came into a clearing that was up a small embankment with a beautiful view of the ocean.

"So," waving his outstretched arms, "what do you think?" Harpreet said with a big smile.

"Beautiful," I nodded with approval, "just beautiful."

Opening up the backpack, Harpreet handed me a paper bag, "Nashta?"

"Nashta?" I asked, "What's nashta?"

"Punjabi lunch," he scowled. "I think Canadians say brunch."

Shaking my head, opening up the bag, "Whatever, I am hungry!"

"I put the food together this morning before leaving for the ferry. It's good, real food, you'll love it."

Nodding in agreement, "Sure thing, because, Harpreet, I love you."

It was indeed lovely, peaceful, and serene. We sat on some second grade, flawed fabric on the grass, eating, talking, and looking over the escarpment to the sparkling sea's skyline. I felt at ease, free, and happy to be back with my love, Harpreet.

How it all came about I don't really recall sequentially. Maybe it was being together after the turbulence of being apart. Or maybe it was the thought of parting again, I don't know, but we decided we would never be apart *again*. One thing seemed to lead to another and we went all Romeo and Juliet.

We simply decided we did not want to live if we could not be together. We knew the way the world worked and we would not be together. So we ripped up the fabrics into a type of rope. We put the noose end around our necks and tipped off the stumps we were standing on.

It happened so fast. I could feel the fabric tighten around my neck, looked over to Harpreet and saw him dangling, but his tree limb was bending and looked like it was starting to break apart. He had such a strange look on his face. Everything went black.

Part Three

Lena Horne said, "It's not the load that breaks you down, it's the way you carry it."

A Fork up the Road – Take It

My telephone was vibrating in my pocket. Pulled it out and answered only to hear, "Help me."

"Shane?"

"Yes Ned, it's me. I need help."

"Okay," I paused a second. "Call display says Vancouver Police Services."

"Fuck that," Shane scoffed, "service is shitty here."

Someone in the background warned, "No profanity please!"

"FUCK YOU!" Shane replied.

The line went dead.

It has been over ten years since the Camp Byng thing. However, Shane was still all fucked up, and he flies the crazy flag accordingly. Finding a dead girl seemed to really mess him up. Uncle R calls it Post Traumatic Stress Disorder—PTSD for short. Even before the Byng thing Shane was weird. Nowadays it's one incident after another.

A couple years ago when we turned nineteen, Logan let on that legally it should be easier to deal with Shane's situations as juvenile emancipation expired. In British Columbia, at age nineteen you are considered an adult. It did not help, and, if anything, made things worse. Adult court was not as lenient as young offenders court. It was an unsightly building, too. Shane was always slugging someone. His fuse was so short that a sideways glance could set Shane off swinging. Another anger management failure to graduate, that's Shane.

Any court appearances required my mum. She's a lawyer, not a criminal lawyer, but better than nothing, and the price was right. My Uncle R usually handled hospital admittances and discharges. Most of the time, however, Shane's fraternal twin sister, Nina, and I would have to arrange bail or apply for a recognizance conditional discharge, or a promise to appear in court. Too bad Shane's record was growing, causing troubles and excessive paperwork. "His record is a metre long!" Logan lamented.

I called Nina; she never picks up, but always responds to my messages later. "Hey Nina, sorry to be calling you about Shane, again. Just got a call from the cop-shop. Don't know what he did this time, but I will see what needs to be done."

Less than ten seconds after calling Nina my phone started ringing. Call display said Vancouver Police Services. "Hello."

The stern voice on the other end said, "Is this Ned Reilly?"

"Yes, it is."

"One moment please."

Turns out the cops dial a number for you if you are incapable of correctly dialing yourself.

"Ned?"

"Hi Shane."

"I'm in the cop shop and need Nina to come and sign me out."

"No problem buddy, I will get Nina. It's happening, straight away, hang in there."

Yes, that is right, one of the innumerable conditions of Shane's probation for who knows which infraction requires that he live with his sister Nina. Just as well, really, who else would or could live with Shane? Nina and Shane rented a townhouse up by the university.

Nina, the polar opposite of Shane, is a pre-med student with a research assistant position and a healthy scholarship.

My phone rang again. It was Nina, "Sorry Ned, I was in the lab when you called, in the middle of mixing test tubes and couldn't pickup."

"No problem Nina, you know anything?"

"No, you?"

"He called from the Police Station and wants you to sign him out."

"Okay, you want to come and get me or shall I come to your place?"

"Oh, well, actually, I've had a beer or two, and probably shouldn't drive." The British Columbia drinking and driving laws had gone off the Richter scale of ridiculously sober. If you've had a drink, or if you know someone who had a drink: Busted.

Nina made a snorting sound, only to say, "On my way, see you in a flash."

Nina is great! Oddly enough she also works with my sister Amelia at UBC. Amelia just turned twenty-five and is setting the world on fire. She is working on a medical degree and law degree concurrently. At first UBC said no, and Amelia would have to choose which degree she wished to pursue, one or the other. Now I have spent my life dealing with Amelia. Ultimatums never work with her. She simply said, "Fine, I will attend the University of Alberta or Seattle instead." UBC caved and Amelia is their ace. Nina is a laboratory coordinator, and is well compensated (according to Amelia).

My grandfather is an anthropologist and I am following in his footsteps. Well, I'm working towards a BA degree. UBC is way more fun than when we went to Jericho Beach High School—not as many rules. JB High was okay, and I survived, but it was just disastrous for Shane. He got suspended, kicked out, and eventually transferred up the road to Dunbar Heights High. Shane hit a teacher. You can't do that.

I could hear that Nina had arrived. She honked her car horn to signal me, and beep beeped again to tell me: "Hurry up." Grabbed my jacket, half a sandwich, and took off to do it all over again.

Thinking to myself, "Shane, what did you do this time?"

Fragile Families &
Fraternal Twins

My brother Shane stirs up shit all the time—what can I do? He's my brother: Stupid Shit and All.

❧

Although I have seen Ned Reilly kicking about for years, and he is one of Shane's best friends, I never actually met his older sister until my interview with the Research Associate Selection Committee. I arrived early, took a seat in the waiting room, and listened to the candidate ahead of me laughing and joking around with the interview committee. Good disengaging skills for sure. The door opened and out came a well-dressed thirty-something handsome man in a blue suit. I looked down at my shoes and thought, "Shit, wish I had dressed up, hadn't even thought about that." The exiting candidate head tilted downward, nodded to me, and briskly walked away. The door to the interview room closed with a slight thunk.

After a few minutes, which seemed more like an eternity, although the clock said otherwise as they were actually right on time, the door opened. An elderly looking white-haired bearded professor emerged. "Hello, are you Kristina Bighill?"

"Yes," I stood to greet him, "Nina, please call me Nina."

"Fine, yes, I am Dr. Dan Adams." Holding out his hand, "Nice to meet you, please come in, meet the committee."

An attractive middle-aged woman with a short blonde hair bob and bright red lips gave me a fist bump. "Hello, I am Lynn Parry."

Smiling I said, "Pleasure to meet you Dr. Parry. Just finished reading your book on Mathematical Biochemistry."

"Oh, don't be such a brown-noser," Amelia Reilly jokingly said as she got up to shake hands. She smiled and said, "Hey, I know you. Didn't you share a placenta with my brother's friend, Shane Bighill?"

"Yes and no," I replied. "Shane is indeed my twin brother, but we are fraternal twins, not sororal twins."

Dr. Adams was making noises and facial expressions to indicate his displeasure with the direction of the introductory discussion. That of course did not dissuade Amelia. "Oh yes, true that, dizygotic DZ twins are offspring produced by the same pregnancy."

"Amelia," Dr. Adams said trying to move the interview along.

"What, this is relevant," Amelia emphasized, "Nina is fraternal not a monozygotic twin. This isn't a random talking point."

"That's right," I confirmed with a nod. "I'm fraternal."

"Yes, yes, fine," Dr. Dan wanted to move along in a different direction. "Amelia, we have a schedule to follow."

"Pitter-patter the schedule does not matter," Amelia was winding up with a boomerang club type thought.

Dr. Parry mediated, putting her hands up saying, "Sorry Amelia, I'm picking up my partner's kid at three and will get injured if I dare to show up late. And you know I am typically a tardy person."

Amelia smiled, and we all sat down to do the interview. Dr. Dan cleared his throat with a startle when Amelia said, "My brother says your brother still *struggles* with the Byng thing."

"No, not really," I had to reply firmly, "I think in terms of working *with* the issues rather than struggles. More positive thinking than anything else."

Dr. Parry sensing a derailment of the three o'clock parameter tried to keep going forward saying, "Okay, lets get started."

Dr. Dan, thinking we've already derailed, and with no concern for the three o'clock pick up time, asked, "Amelia, given these circumstances, I wonder whether you should recuse on this interview?"

"No, no, no," I blurted, "Dr. Dan, I can't believe you would suggest such a situation."

Amelia got all frown-like. "Nina, your thoughts?" Amelia asked.

"Sorry Amelia," a reluctant Lynn Parry interjected, "I'm afraid Ms. Bighill's thoughts do not count in this situation."

"*Hey, no way,*" I said a little louder than likely needed. "My thoughts certainly count."

Dr. Dan gets up and says, "Yes, of course, your thoughts count. However, would you please just give us the room for a moment to caucus?"

"No, there's no caucusing," I said assertively.

"I agree," Amelia piped in, "no need to recuse nor caucus. Let's get going on the interview."

"Agreed." I said with some emphasis and a head nod to everyone respectively.

"Amelia, do you not see any reason to recuse?" Dr. Dan asked.

"No," Amelia said with some level of hostility, "I do not need to recuse!"

"Fine," he looked over to me, "Ms. Bighill are you satisfied that Ms. Reilly does not hold any bias towards your application?"

Scrunched my face and said, "No, there is no bias *evident.*" Looking around the table, I explained, "I would be more dissatisfied if the interview was adjourned. Shall we get started?"

The committee looked at each other and Dr. Dan said, "Yes, indeed, we should get started."

An Ocean of Diarrhea

My sister works with Ned's sister. Seems they are both big-time university nerds. Guess they are smart. Dunno, cuz it doesn't matter, Nina is my twin sister and I've known her all my life. We shared a womb, at the same time. Ned's sister, Amelia, is three years older than us, but that means nothing anyways. Actually, nothing means nothing these days. Its all shit.

I've always said my friend Ned is an island of reality in an ocean of diarrhea. Ned is the nicest guy I know. If you ever need help, call Ned.

Ned's uncle said it was a *"conflict"* and he couldn't be my shrink. I didn't like the first court appointed shrink, she sucked, and they had to settle on selecting a new shrink. I knew I needed a shrink, but I wanted a nice one, not an asshole.

Dr. Lisa Rae came to visit me when I was in the hospital. The cops put a beating on me cuz they said I didn't "follow their orders." Who the fucks were they to be ordering me around anyways, I hadn't done nothing wrong.

She slid into the hospital room without making much noise. I saw her, and she knew it, but when she moved the chair in the corner to sit beside me, it made a terrible sound. "Sorry, Shane," she said, "Were you resting?"

"Well, wasn't dancing," I replied with a wink.

"Okay, hello, I am Dr. Rae. Did anyone tell you I was coming to see you today?"

"No one tells me shit!"

"Okay, well, that changes now," she said nodding her head and pulling out a note pad. "Dr. Reilly says you are a friend of his."

"Yeah, he's Ned's uncle," I confirmed. "Your name Ray like ray of sunshine?" I asked.

"No, not really," she smiled. "I spell my name R-A-E, no Y. But, you can call me Lisa."

"Fine, okay, listen Lisa," I raised my hand, "Can you get me out of here?"

"Yes, of course, that is the plan," she said with a nodding head.

"Whose plan?" I asked.

"Our plan," she said furrowing her brow. "Of course, your compliance and cooperation is what it is all about. You are in charge Shane."

"Doesn't feel like I am in charge of fucking anything. Can I get up and leave. No, I already know the door at the end of the hall is locked."

"Yes, that is true," she said bobbing her head. "In addition to some medical concerns, you have a few legal issues that need to be resolved."

"Yeah, like what?" I asked.

"I don't know details about all of the legal issues. I'm not a lawyer. However, I met with your sister, Nina, and Dr. Reilly this morning. They say you have secured legal representation. I understand Nina and your friend Ned were here earlier this morning, but I guess you were still sedated and sleeping."

"Yeah, who said they could sedate me?"

"Yes, good question, and that is one of the issues we are working on."

"Who's this *we* you are talking about Miss Shrink Lady?"

"You and I, Shane. We are working on the issues. And you can call me Lisa."

"Lisa, what makes you think I want you to be my shrink?"

She opened up her bag and pulled out some papers. "Yes, now that you mention it Shane. I have some consent forms for you to sign to inform the court that I will serve as your court appointed psychologist."

"What if I don't sign 'em?"

"No problem, if you do not wish to sign the consent forms, the court will need to find another psychologist for you to work with."

"Can I think about it?"

Smiling and more head bobs, Lisa started stuffing the papers back into her bag. "Yes, you should think about things Shane. I will come back tomorrow and we can talk further, if you wish."

She got up and started to walk away. "Hey Lisa, are you a busy shrink?"

Another smile with a head bob, "Yes, I have a very busy practice. Why do you ask? Are you concerned I will not make you a priority?"

"Naw, nothing like that. My sister Nina, who is the smartest person I know, next to Ned, always says: If you want to get something done ask a busy person to do it. That's cuz the people who are not busy are not busy for a reason. Get it?"

"Yes, Shane, I get it, see you tomorrow."

"Okay, super shrink, see ya tomorrow."

Soon as she left the hospital room fuckers come in trying to give me more meds. At first I politely declined the meds. And then I had to ask, "Buddy, you like sex and travel?"

"Excuse me, come again, sex and travel."

"Yeah, sex and travel, that means FUCK OFF!"

It didn't work. The fat guy pinned one arm and the ugly, stinky guy grabbed the other, and then the nurse jabbed me with a big honking needle. Ouch. Everything went dark.

Sure as shit the next day Lisa shows up, slides in to my room, pulls up a chair and asks, "How are you today Shane?"

"Dunno, feeling fucked up, what are they giving me? Everything is all blurry and brackish, but you aren't. You look good. Nice tits. Do people tell you that you have nice tits?"

"Thanks Shane, try and focus on our problems."

"What problems you got Lisa?"

"Well, this morning your lawyers looked after one problem for us."

"Yeah, what problem was that, and who are my lawyers?"

She seemed to look surprised, started flipping through her note pad, found the page she wanted, and said, "Jedd Talbot and Annette Reilly have been retained by your sister to serve as your lawyers. The first thing they did this morning was to secure a court order preventing any further forced sedation on you."

"That's good," I nodded with approval. "Annette is Ned's mum and she works for free. Who's the other guy?"

Lisa peered down her nose at me, "Jedd Talbot is a very expensive, high profile lawyer. I can assure you he doesn't work for free."

"Too bad cuz I don't have any money."

Another smile, "Someone does, and it appears they are preparing criminal charges against you."

"That's nothing Lisa, they're always charging me with something. They trump this shit up, you know. Cops say I am *known to them*."

"Yes, I know."

"Hey, who's paying the bill for you? And how much do you cost?" I asked.

Still smiling and pulling out papers, "Don't worry about my fees Shane. If you wish to sign these consent forms, the court will cover the costs."

"Shit yeah, pass them over, I'll sign." And that was that, I had a new super shrink. A nice one, too.

Dr. R ~
Competence & Confidence

Michelle Obama cautioned Golden State's Steph Curry, "You think long you think wrong."

⚘

Irrespective of whether it is a formal dictate or popular parlance in psychology, One's competence is paramount. You *must* be confident of your competence. Confidence takes you some distance, but the Punjabi saying: *Easy to Say, Hard to Do* is often too true in confidence terms.

Many years ago, when I was a young psychologist, I was oh so ever confident. I had a freshly printed psychologist's license and was ready to practice. Problems, big or small, I was ready for them all.

Now I am older, maybe a little more humble, certainly less confident. Maybe I did not know as much as I once thought. Diagnosing wasn't as easy and straightforward. Patients or parents did not want to hear me say: "She's a GORK."

"A GORK?"

Yes, that was my diagnosis. I had administered a comprehensive battery of standard and nonstandardized scales, analyzed the results and derived a diagnosis of GORK. That is, **G**od **O**nly **R**eally **K**nows what is wrong with her. I don't.

"Here's your bill."

"You think insurance will cover this."

"Yes, no problem."

B.F. Skinner was the most notable preeminent psychological theorist to say: "I knew as I was aging my cognitive capabilities were diminishing, but my wisdom was increasing."

I have known Shane Bighill since he was a kid in Cub Scouts. I was there when Shane discovered the body of Banerjee Malik swinging from a tree just outside the Camp Byng property. Her suicide weighed heavy on all of us, but Shane took it particularly hard. He thought if only he had gotten there sooner the whole thing could have been prevented.

Eighteen-year-old Banerjee had entered a suicide pact with her nineteen year old boyfriend, Harpreet Dhaliwal. They had tied makeshift fabric ropes around their necks, fastened the ends to tree branches, faced each other and jumped off stumps. Harpreet's weight broke the branch. He lived, but had massive brain damage due to the period of time where his brain did not receive oxygen.

In point of fact, the boys actually saved Harpreet's life. If they hadn't shown up when they did, Harpreet would have certainly died. It was the middle of nowhere on the Gibsons coastline.

The boys were eleven years old and we were at the Boy Scouts Camp Byng Spring Campout. I was supposed to be the "responsible adult" chaperoning my nephew Ned and his three friends: Shane, Raj, and Logan.

The immediate fallout after the boys discovered Harpreet and Banerjee was heavy. My sister is Ned's mother, and is a prominent lawyer (she tells us so all the time). However, my wife is an Appeals Court Judge. Sometimes their opinions converge and diverge. And I attempt to interpret the in between legal nuances. My sister Annette lit her hair on fire (metaphorically speaking) about the idea of adolescent posttraumatic stress disorder (PTSD). It was difficult for her to understand the repercussions and psychological implications. My wife, Harjit, was helpful, but it was hard.

The boys desperately wanted to attend Banerjee's funeral. The boys' respective parents were of varying opinions. Nevertheless, Harjit and I approached Banerjee's family with the request of the boys' attendance at the funeral service. Their request was forcefully declined.

We explained to the boys that Banerjee's family was sad and mad, but bottom line was the boys would not be welcome at the service. It was a *private family* event. In turn, the boys became sad and mad.

Harpreet became their next obsession. They were fixated on where Harpreet was and was he going to die. When can they see him? They saved him and they *deserved* to see him!

Eleven-year-old boys present challenges at the best of times, and, of course, the challenges accelerate during the worst of times. My sister was against everything and I understood that. Annette can be difficult. Nevertheless, my wife and I approached Harpreet's family under the auspices of being helpful in *their* time of need.

Mrs. Dhaliwal was marvelous. She cried and cried extensively, but the idea that my nephew saved her son's life made him a hero in her eyes. She was grateful that Harpreet was still alive, albeit in serious life threatening condition in the Vancouver General Hospital's Intensive Care Unit. No one could visit him in the ICU. Even so "Yes, yes, yes, of course, when Harpreet is moved to the other hospital ward the boys may certainly visit. That would be very nice," said Mrs. Dhaliwal. "I would like that."

And so the boys VGH visits began. Again, not all the parents were onside with this visitation idea and we received some telephone calls, emails and heavy front door knockings. Eventually, Harry was moved to a regular VGH room and along with Mrs. Dhaliwal we went as a group to visit.

"Harpreet has massive brain damage," the resident physician explained to the boys upon our first visit. "We are monitoring his condition, and a comprehensive prognosis is difficult to articulate."

All the boys can hear, but not all listen. "When's he gonna start talking?"

Shane asked. "We got questions."

"They are not exactly sure at this point, Shane." I tried to explain. Made it worse by adding, "Harpreet has brain damage and may never talk or walk again."

"*What!*" The boys reacted poorly to this information.

Being correct is more important to my sister than me. Being correct can be a burden. And so it was dealing with the boys and Harpreet's prognosis. At first, every day after school the boys rode their bikes to the hospital to visit Harry. They did this on their own. As I explained to my sister, I had no part to play in arranging or participating in subsequent visitations. "Boys will be boys."

Some weeks passed and Harpreet was released from hospital and sent home to live with his parents. Indeed, he could not walk or talk, but was alive and living. Harpreet was an invalid. The boys began visiting him at home and both Mrs. Dhaliwal and Harry were always happy to see them. Harry could smile.

Logan Meyers's parents retained an expensive psychotherapist to assist with his recovery. *You can lead a horse to water, but you cannot make him drink.* Logan and his family had other issues besides the critical incident where Logan and Shane first discovered Banny and Harpreet. Logan was angry with his parents over who knows what, and his parents had never dealt adequately with the death of their oldest son, Benjamin. Of course, I agree, family therapy was a good idea, but I understand there were issues and difficult times. Nevertheless, the famous Dr. E. did agree that the boys' visitations to the hospital might prove productive in their psychological recoveries.

Once Logan had permission to visit Harpreet at the hospital the other parents fell in line and come rain or shine the boys showed up in full force. They continued visits when Harpreet was moved to live at home with his parents. I drove Ned a few times when it was raining. It rains a lot in Vancouver.

Raj Gill's Coming Home

Hit me with lightning, burn me with BTUs, when I heard about Shane I couldn't believe it. No way, it's not true.

I was going to the University of Chandigarh in Northern India's Punjab region when my sister called to give me the news. There is a twelve-hour time difference between Vancouver and India, but that means nothing to my sister.

"WTF," I sort of screamed at Parminder. The time difference makes my attitude difficult. "Shane has been arrested for murder?"

"Yes, just saw it on the six o'clock news," Parminder said whistling for emphasis.

"What are they saying?"

Parm whistled *again*. "Well, first, they did a perp walk, and Shane looked pretty rough. Now your friend Ned Reilly's mum is being interviewed.

Now she's backing off and according to the television's caption, some guy named Jedd Talbot is speaking. He's handsome."

"Shit-a-brick, Jedd Talbot's Shane's lawyer?" I asked.

"Yes, that's what it says on TV. You know Jedd Talbot?"

"You don't!"

"Nope, who is he?"

"Jedd Talbot is one of the biggest criminal defence lawyers in Vancouver! Shane is in some shit if Talbot's his lawyer!"

"Yeah, guess so, he's charged with murder." Parminder whistled, yet again.

"Okay Parm," I whistled back at her. "I'm on the next flight out of here. Please call Ned Reilly or Logan Meyers. They need to know I am coming home."

"Really," Parm sounded perplexed. "You are dropping everything and coming home?"

"Yes, no choice Parm," I started crying. "It's Shane, for fuck sake. It's Shane! Call Ned and Logan, okay?"

"Yes, okay Raj, I'm on it. See you soon."

Internalizing ~ Logan's Lament

Shane always had issues! This is nothing new. Ever since we were little kids, Shane has had problems. Even so, after *we* found Banerjee swinging from a tree, Shane was never the same. I tried talking to him about the whole thing. After all, it was *me*; I was there with him. We found her *together*. We saved Harry. Everybody knows that is true. Shane couldn't shake the whole thing off his shoulders. He just kept getting worse and worse. He started doing stupid stuff *all the time!*

Ned understood. I became an internalizer. Shane became an externalizer. I was quite contained and a bit bottled up while Shane exploded and fucked up all over the place all the time.

We didn't lose Shane overnight or anything like that. It took a while. He started smoking too much weed, drinking beer, and was angry all the time. He spazzed out over nothing, he'd get all shrill like, and one time he punched me in the face.

"Shane, you fucking asshole!" Ned screamed at him. "You punched Logan in the face!"

"I did," Shane shook his head. "Yes, I did."

"Why?"

"Dunno," Shane shrugged. "Logan's always bugging me."

"So what!" Ned pushed him. "You can't punch Logan!"

My therapist suggested Shane's anger issues directed towards me were expressed because we were both together when we found Banerjee. Or, something like that. "It's complicated."

I started to lose track of Shane. Mostly, however, I think once Raj moved to university in India our little group fell apart. Well, that is, until Shane got arrested and put in jail, charged with murder.

Raj flew back home. Ned and I met him at the airport.

Westport Road to the Fintry Estate

Nina was born first, and about eight minutes later Shane was born. Although merely holding a father's standing, I cut both umbilical cords. Of course, no dispute needed, it was different for Connie. She's the mum, carried them for nine months, and brought them out of the womb safely. All I did was cut the cords.

I became the father of fraternal twins. Certainly told them, Connie, and anyone else who'd listen, "Don't worry, I'll do my best to take care of you."

God knows, Buddha, Zeus and Aphrodite all could see I was always trying to keep Shane's head above the waterline. Nina didn't need me; she walked on water, and with style, too.

Again, as I said, I cut both umbilical cords, hence I know where they came from and, of course, we expected some differences. They were fraternal not identical twins. Just didn't expect such marked differences to emerge early and carry on so long. Shane seemed to show a high maintenance schedule from the beginning. Of course, everything turned upside down when Shane and his friends found a dead girl outside Gibsons. He was only eleven years old.

Age thirteen was Shane's first brush with the law. He got caught shoplifting chocolate bars from a grocery store during the school lunch break. "He had a twenty dollar bill in his pocket!" Nina, who was first on the scene, screamed at me over the telephone.

"Okay, Nina, I'm on my way, it'll be okay." I assured her, but she seemed to know better. Connie and I hoped for the best.

Age fourteen some teacher said something Shane took exception to and he cold-cocked him in the classroom. When Vice Principal Greenstreet arrived on the scene to see what was going on, Shane slugged her, too. He subsequently got suspended from school. Shortly thereafter he got expelled from Jericho Beach High School for threatening the principal's life.

Our lawyer was able to negotiate a transfer to another school up the road, Dunbar Heights High School. Shane assured us he would do better, and he did, for a while.

Age fifteen Shane stole a car and crashed it into a tree. "They left the keys in the ignition, and it was raining." Shane explained as though it was not really his fault. "Nobody got hurt."

A series of pedestrian, but annoying legal infractions occurred on a semi-regular basis. Although it was difficult for everyone involved, Connie always took it hard. She tried to hide her crying with little success. "A mother cannot compartmentalize the way you can!"

"Connie, that's not fair."

"What is fair?"

❧

We were scheduled to attend a family celebration at Connie's brothers house overlooking the lake outside West Kelowna. Their father had been receiving chemotherapy treatments and we were celebrating the news that the treatments had done their job, "Grampa's doctors say he is now *cancer free!*"

It was the Queen Victoria Day long weekend. I had recently purchased a new Porsche 911 Boxster. An *entry level* Porsche for sixty thousand not like the one Connie's brother drove that cost close to two hundred thousand. I'm modest enough not to sink too much money into our *second* car. Connie drives an old Mercedes. She likes it and doesn't like changes.

We got an early start Friday morning because we knew the traffic getting out of Vancouver would be tough. It was. Took the Princeton to Penticton Highway in order to see some sights and give the car a little workout on the curves. It was a lovely day, lots of sunshine, but not too hot.

We were about five and a half hours into the trip, almost there, when it happened. It is true; your life does pass before your eyes before you die! Everything was in such slow motion. I saw it unfolding so slowly.

We were travelling up the two-lane mountain road on the way towards the Fintry Estate and Provincial Park. I could see her coming down the road towards us in a white pickup truck. She was going too fast, lost control, fish tailed, and then crossed the centre line and hit us *head on*. The noise was loud and the smells were pungent. I looked over to Connie. She was gone. It was over, and this was how it ended.

"I'm sorry Connie," I croaked, but knew she couldn't hear me. I was slowly bleeding out, growing cold, and blurry, thinking "Oh shit, Shane. Who's going to look out for Shane?"

Firefighters and the Jaws of Life arrived. I was still alive at that point, but sliding fast.

"Hold on buddy."

The lady firefighter asked, "Sir, can you hear me sir?"

I whispered, "Nina, someone has to call Nina."

That was it, and it was over.

All I could think of was, "Nina you are in charge now."

"Sorry."

Nina Never Lets Go

"I'd like to think the best of me still hiding up my sleeve." ~John Mayer, *Room for Squares*

❦

My brother's friend, Ned Reilly, is the epitome of reliability. You can count on Ned. It has become an empirical fact Ned's got Shane's back. And now I know he has mine, too. Its good to have him in our corner, we need the help. Our parents died in a car accident when we were eighteen.

Just to make things even odder, three years later, I am working with Ned's sister, Amelia. It is a small world after all. Six degrees of separation as an algorithm explains a lot. I was learning to love applied mathematics. "Yes," I nodded, "agreed, that is a beautiful equation."

Age twenty-one and I landed my dream job in Amelia's UBC lab. The pay is fantastic with some flexible hours and there is no doubt we are in line to win a Nobel Prize. This is as good as it gets. "Scientific strides and threshold thrashings, that's what we're doing in this lab," Amelia said on my first day, along with a heavy fist pump.

"Okay, let's get started."

Six months later we were on the verge of a major breakthrough. The corner of the lab where my workstation was located looks after the DNA decomposition protocols with carcinogens and pathogens, both synthetic and organic. The tech guys were in again today installing software. Sometimes it was good and sometimes just more of the same stuff but more complicated. Now when someone dials my lab line a message appears across all my platforms.

I was in the middle of a timed experiment when I saw Ned's message. "Hey Nina, sorry to be calling about Shane again. Don't know what he did this time, but I will see what needs to be done."

Ned handled as many of Shane's episodes as possible. However, a current condition clause in Shane's probation agreement was that he lives with me and I held signing authority over his situation. As soon as I could I gave Ned a call. "Sorry Ned, I was in the lab when you called, in the middle of mixing test tubes, and couldn't pick up."

"No problem Nina, you know anything?"

"No, you?"

"He called from the Police Station and wants you to sign him out."

"Okay, you want to come and get me or shall I come to your place?"

"Oh, well, I've had a beer or two, and probably shouldn't drive."

I chuckled out loud, "On my way, see you in a flash." Got my stuff together, shut down systems into sleep mode, and drove down to lower Wallace Street where Ned lives.

Usually Ned is already standing on the side of the road waiting for me. Didn't see him so I gave the horn a little honk to let him know I had arrived. No action, so I beep beeped again.

The front door opened and Ned came flying out, half a sandwich in his mouth, putting on a rain jacket at the same time. "Oh man, more rain!" Ned moaned, climbing into the car. "Just spoke with my mum and she knows nothing about Shane's charges tonight."

"Maybe there are no charges, maybe they just arrested him again for being obnoxious," I wondered out loud.

"Maybe."

True enough, this night, we got to the Police Station and Shane was waiting for us, sitting in a holding area. I signed some papers and they released him into our stewardship.

Three days later at two in the morning a group of detectives and some uniformed cops showed up at our door with a warrant for Shane's arrest. Evidently, they now had enough to charge him with the murders of Trent McKinney and Declan Downes.

Shane was sound asleep when I had to rouse him from his bed. The cops were right behind me, put him in handcuffs, and took him away in an unmarked car.

I called Ned.

Dr. Lisa ~
Super Shrink & Shane

"Givers have to set limits because takers rarely do." ~Henry Ford

※

We had just returned home from Saskatchewan, I was tired, and the absolute last thing I wanted was a new referral, but I got a call from the famous Dr. Randal Reilly asking for a *"favour."* Actually, it's his wife, Judge Harjit Singh, who holds a higher level of fame, but Randal's okay. I had met him a couple times at psychology board functions.

Judge Singh heard the *Meyers vs. Shuster* case. My then girlfriend, Mavis was a junior lawyer on the Meyers side. We were young and in love. I went to the courtroom every day just to watch Mavis sit as second chair. It made her feel supported having me in the gallery. She didn't do much as a junior lawyer, but she'd turn around every now and then to wink at me. I always thought, "What's with the winking."

The case was about ten-year old Benji Meyers who had been seriously, well, actually, fatally injured in a bicycle accident. Benji was brain dead and the family had decided to *pull-the-plug* and take Benji off life support systems. They went so far as to bring little brother

Logan to the hospital to say goodbye. Logan had a bad reaction. The Meyers' then offered Benji's grandparents the same opportunity to visit the hospital. Both pairs of grandparents showed up at the same time. "If you think little Logan had a bad reaction, the Shusters, grandparents on the mother's side, went all weird and got their lawyer to file an injunction to prevent Benji's *medically-assisted-death."*

The trial lasted three days. Both sides had experts giving their opinions on what they thought should ultimately be the disposition of Benji Meyers. Judge Singh listened to all of the testimonies and arguments for and against keeping Benji alive hooked up to life support systems. At the end of the third day Judge Singh adjourned for the day, reserving her decision, which would be delivered in two days.

Mavis went all wingy waiting on pins and needles for Judge Singh's decision. Her anxiety was contagious and I always got sucked into her drama. On the day the decision was to be delivered Mavis was all wound up, nervous, and driving me nuts. I drove to the court-house, dropped her off, and said I'd meet her inside. Thought about driving away and leaving Mavis behind, but that would be less than classy. I waited a week to dump her.

Judge Singh decided it would be "in Benji's *best interests* to with-draw the life support systems." It took another two days for him to die.

Mavis' side *won,* and winning was everything for Mavis. She looked forward to the day when she would sit *first* chair. We both knew it was time to move on and I had to frame my departure in such a way that Mavis did not feel like a loser. First chair, second chair, I didn't care, our relationship had run its course.

Hard to believe, but sixteen years have flown by since the Meyers case, and what do you know, I get a call from Dr. Randal Reilly asking for a *favour.* "We need a forensic psychologist to do a fitness for trial assessment. Hope you can help us out."

Of course, although I am busier than I wish, I took a meeting with Dr. Reilly and Nina Bighill. Seems Shane Bighill, who suffers from a shopping list of problems, was arrested, released, and re-arrested. While he was being re-arrested the police put a bit of a beating on him and now Shane is out on bail in a hospital room. The court wants to know if Shane is fit to stand trial.

The first time I met Shane we discussed a few issues centered around forced medication and sedation due to perceived aggressiveness on Shane's part. I gave him a basic Mental Status Exam, but before we could progress further Shane wanted to think further about whether he would consent to my seeing him as a patient.

The second session the next day Shane was coming down from forced sedation that was now prohibited by a court order. The hospital staff could no longer forcefully sedate Shane. His legal team successfully acquired an injunction and Shane could no longer be held in hospital without consent. He seemed happy to sign my required assessment consent forms.

Shane calls me his super shrink.

Uncle R ~ Best Friends Ever

"When it is raining, let your smile be the umbrella." ~Douglas J. Mc-Nicol, (1955 – 2016) CUPE 1004

❧

"Ned, I've never had friends like the ones I had when I was twelve," Uncle R said while we were eating Whitespot burgers and poutine fries with gravy. "You'll see what I mean when you're older."

All my life Uncle R has always said this sort of stuff. Sure, when I get older life will look different. Yes, profound enough, but I knew he was likely on to something. When I think of Raj, Logan, and Shane these guys have been my friends since we were little kids. I'm turning twenty-two.

Uncle R glanced at his wrist clock, "Logan's late?"

"Yeah."

"What do you think that means?"

"Means he's late."

Uncle R nodded, smiled and said, "Logan's never late."

"Yeah, I know."

"You worried about him?"

I just started crying right then and there in the stupid Whitespot Restaurant. Not full fledged bawling my brains out crying, just soft whimpers with tears and sniffles.

Uncle R reached over touching my hand, "Hey, hey, hey, its going be okay."

"No!" I burst out into another wave of whimpers, "its *not* gonna be okay. Everything's all fucked up."

Uncle R did some deep sighs and said, "We're just going have to go one step at a time and see where it all leads."

"You think Shane *killed* those two guys?"

"No!" Uncle R winced. "No way, not our Shane! Its all a big mistake and it'll get straighten out. Don't worry. The cops always make mistakes."

Looking through the window I could see Logan was walking towards the restaurant. Quickly pulling myself together, I said, "Logan's here."

"Alright!" Uncle R smiled. "I knew everything was okay."

Logan came inside, looked around, saw me waving and came to the booth. "Shove over fatso," he said sliding in beside me.

"How you doing, Logan?" Uncle R asked.

"Parking's a bugger, traffic sucks and school's piling on crap," he fist bumped Uncle R. "Otherwise I'm okay."

"You're never late." I pointed my index finger at him.

"First time for everything there sporty," Logan said, elbowing me in the ribs. "Don't sweat the small stuff. What time does Raj's plane land?"

"Eight."

"Great, we've got plenty of time. Uncle R you coming to the airport?"

I answered for him, "No, its you and me, remember."

"Okay, we can go in my car."

"Logan, that was the plan all along," I reminded him.

"Right, right, yes, that's why I'm meeting you and Uncle R here. I knew that."

"Logan you're acting weird, everything okay?"

"What, I'm not acting weird, this is how I am. You think I'm weird."

Uncle R and I answer in unison, "Yeah, Logan, you *are* weird!"

"Oh well," Logan shrugged, "at least I'm good looking."

"Says who?" I asked with a smile. I was feeling better now; Mr. Suave and Sophisticated was here.

"Your Mama," Logan laughed, "that's who says I'm good looking!"

We just shook our heads, Uncle R paid the bill—he gets all uppity if I try to pay so I don't even bother anymore. We did some hugs and shoulder slugs in the parking lot and drove away in different directions.

Punjab to Vancouver

After the 2016 election Barack Obama told his disappointed daughters, "The end of the world is the end of the world. This isn't the end of the world." #GreatFathers

※

Takes half a day to fly from the Punjab to Vancouver. Takes a few more days to recover from jetlag. My father telephoned the Punjab *twice* to let me know his disapproval. Evidently, Parminder let him know my travel plans. Pop does not respond well to surprises. His denunciation of my decision was to be expected. "So you are throwing your education away? For what?"

"No dad, I am not *throwing* my education away." I tried to explain, "I'm taking a break."

"Oh, you need a break?"

"Yes, I need a break."

"Oh, university is too hard so you need a break."

"Farthest from the truth dad," I snorted. "You saw my grades. You think you could do better?" I earned close to perfect grades and he knew it.

"Oh, oh, ohhhh," he moaned, "I am no quitter, you say."

"Not quitting dad, taking a break." Now I knew nothing could be said to appease dad, but disconnecting would send him through the stratosphere of anger mis-management. "Gotta go dad, see you soon." I hung up.

In between dad's diatribes Logan called to let me know he and Ned would meet me at the airport. "Perfect timing Raj," Logan proclaimed. Wendy just moved out so there is lots of space at my place."

Logan's father is a moneyman who owns houses and apartment buildings everywhere. "Sorry Logan," I sighed. "Wendy dumped you?"

"Ned told you?"

"No, *you* just told me."

"Yes, well, its over now," Logan moaned. "For real, this time, I think."

"What happened?" I asked cajolingly.

Logan chuckled, "Usual shit, Wendy said I was too contained, uptight, unimaginative and boring."

"Bummer."

"My feet were cold so I wore white socks with sandals. Wendy went nuts on me."

"Fashion faux pas?"

"Yes, one of too many."

I knew true enough that Wendy was a little dominating, but Logan has his issues, too. They hit a BIG bump in the road when Logan let Shane stay in the basement for what was supposed to only be for a little while. Of course, didn't take Shane long to wear out his welcome. He smoked too much weed, drank too much beer, made too much noise, always made a mess in the kitchen and always walked around naked.

The authorities forced Shane to move out of Logan's basement and start living with Nina as a condition of his probation. Ned's mum, the lawyer, negotiated the clause under the auspices of "family supervision". No supervision at Logan's and after Shane started a fight and busted up the Arbutus Street Pub, he was arrested. Someone said something he didn't like. "They caused it!" According to Shane.

When Wendy wanted Logan to choose between Shane or her because "One of us has to go!" Socks and sandals notwithstanding, Logan would never turn his back on Shane.

Never.

❧

"Logan," I had to ask, "You think Shane killed those guys?"

"Shit Raj," Logan started to rant out on me. "No, not Shane, he didn't do it! Ned says doesn't matter, its Shane. Our Shane."

"Okay, got it, see you soon." No sense getting into things with Logan, but in my head I had to wonder. Shane does do weird shit. Who knows?

Calming Down – R. Fabbro's Song

In the history of calming down nobody ever calmed down when they were told to calm down. I tried to explain this to Parminder. She felt bad to hear her father and brother squabbling on the telephone. She felt responsible because Raj told her he was leaving university in India to come and be with his friend Shane. She told father and father went crazy. "Papa ji, please calm down," Parminder pleaded. It was no use.

I understood Raj. If Shane had died, Raj would have come back for the funeral. Father could say nothing on that account. "But this is different!" husband screams at me. "Shane did not die. He killed two people!"

Fathers and sons, I do not understand. My father and brother were the same. Now I hear husband and my son Raj doing this thing. Why? It is no good.

Parminder is in her room crying. Husband stomping around angry, for what? And me, I cannot wait to see my son Raj. He is coming home. Of course, I am happy, cannot say so, but I am happy. He is my boy. And, yes, he is a *blessing!* Just the same as my right hand is important, but no more than my left hand. They are the same. Raj is a blessing.

My boy.

Jedd Talbot ~
Messages, Numbers & Omens

A long time ago, back when I held only one email and one cellular number, life was simpler. Nowadays seems like no end to the number of numbers plaguing me on so many levels. Colleagues, junior lawyers, paralegals, secretaries and so many more are calling, texting, emailing and PDF-ing me incessantly. However, my original number is controlled by me and me alone.

Two Voicemail Messages: One was from the Cancer Clinic and the other read Annette Reilly. I knew what the Cancer Clinic call was about, but my memory was failing. "Who is Annette Reilly? The name sounds familiar, and how did she get this number?"

I skipped the Cancer message and pushed the button to hear her message. "Hello Mr. Talbot, this is Annette Reilly calling. We met briefly at the Karl Holmes party. My son Ned serves as a *roadie* or a gopher for the *Mahjeeroms* whenever they are in town. His father, Thomas, is a guitar player. Thomas gave me your number."

Smiling to myself, yes, I remembered, Karl's party. Great party! I was everyone's hero, especially Karl. I landed the *Mahjeeroms* to play for a private party—Karl's party.

"Mr. Talbot, I need some help. Your name was suggested as someone who could sit first-chair in a criminal case against my son's friend, Shane Bighill."

Now, his name seemed familiar, too. Shane Bighill, where have I heard that name?

"Please call me at your convenience and I can supply further details. Thanks."

Didn't delete the cancer message, just skipped it. *Mahjeeroms* are the best. I started to feel a little weepy. Thought a little bit of a cry was coming on so I called Ms. Reilly straight away. It's an omen.

Defensive coping mechanisms—got a million of them.

Fucking cancer folks can wait.

Sad, Mad, and/or Glad

"Ma, how long you think Pops and Raj will carry on this stupid feud?" I asked while we were driving our old minivan to Logan Meyers' house. "This not talking, not seeing each other is too ridiculous, eh?"

Pursing her lips, and shrugging, "Mennu putt anni," was the best she could say.

"I don't know, either." Although Ma's English is very good, she speaks Punjabi when she is sad or mad. Actually, come to think of it, she speaks Punjabi when she is glad, too.

Today she is all three: sad, mad, and glad. She's glad because we are on our way to see Raj at Logan Meyers' house. We've got a minivan full of food in tiffin containers, and Tupperware. We've got trinkets and tchotchkes, too. The boys love Ma's cooking. Rotis, chapattis, dhal, curry and saags are fantastic favourites. The boys are going over to Ned Reilly's Uncle's cottage on Mayne Island. Ma received a green light to deliver a care package for the boys.

She is sad because her baby boy, Raj, is twenty-two years old and he has elected to live with Logan. "He does not live at home with his family anymore."

She is mad because Raj and Pops are bickering. "They are both so stupor!"

Pulling into Logan's driveway we could see a good crowd had already arrived and were milling about out front. "Oh that Nina Bighill has become beautiful." Ma moaned, pointing at Shane's sister. "Look at that other girl. What is she wearing?"

"No finger pointing, Ma!" I tried to remind her about good manners.

"Oh-my-goodness, look at that Ned Reilly. He has gotten so tall."

"Yes Ma, Ned's six-foot small." I chuckled.

The finger of doom turned to point at me, "No smarty-girl stuff, eh!"

Fortunately the gang descended upon us before Ma could get worked up over *smarty-girl stuff.* Ned approached the minivan with his hands clasped together. "Sats ri akal, Mrs. Gill. Twadda kee haul hay."

Ma likes it and tee-hee-hees, smiles, and giggles whenever Ned speaks Punglish to her. His aunt taught him some vocabulary words and he has Punjabi language books. Raj says Ned speaks a combo of Punjabi and English. Hence, he speaks *Punglish.*

We started unloading the stockpile of cargo. Shane sauntered over and took a large load. "Cool wheels, Parminder."

"Yeah, Ma's old Toyota minivan. She loves it, nothing like it."

"Nothing wrong!" Shane knew Ma's slogan. Then he opened a container and started eating. "Yum, these pakoras are good!"

Shaking her head, Nina said, "Shane!"

"What?" Shane smiled. "I love Mrs. Gill's pakoras!"

If Looks Could Kill

My mum is the master of dirty looks. Her stink eye throws theta waves right at you, according to my sister Amelia (a theta wave expert). We were a dinner quartet at the Topanga Cafe on fourth when Uncle R suggested to Nina, "You should take Shane over to my sea-shack on Mayne Island for a week or so. Get him out of town for a while. The island would be a perfect place for him to unwind. He needs to relax before the trial"

Mum pivoted, and turned to Uncle R saying, "Where do you come up with these brain waves? Get Shane out of town?"

"Yes, Annette, think about it. It's a relatively small island. He can't get into trouble there. Other than he likes to tip his kayak, but that's another story altogether." Uncle R said with a smile and a wink to me.

"What do you mean, he likes to *tip his kayak*? Nina asked.

Answering for Uncle R, I explained, "Ever since we were Cub Scouts we always talk about the kayak Inuit Roll. Shane's the only one who always goes through with it, for real. I always duck out saying the water is too cold. Not Shane. Cold water is not a big deal for him."

Shaking her head, "I hate cold water," fraternal twin sister Nina said with a scowl.

"Shane has bail conditions!" Mum emphasized, a little more forcefully than required.

Nina nodded, smiled, and said, "I'll talk to him, tomorrow."

Trying to Square the Circle

"How old would you be if you didn't know your age?" said Coquitlam's Christine Lauzon.

࿔

Logan slowly inhales deeply, and starts to explain; "When I was seventeen my therapist suggested it was now time I made peace with mother. Dad was doing the best he could with me, but easily capitulated to anything the therapist recommended. So, sure I went to Seattle to stay with mother. After all, it was likely time to make peace."

Although I actually did like attending South Seattle's Rainer Beach High School, it's always been hard living with mother. After six months or so, it is hard to remember the actual disengaging detonating point; we both knew things were not going to work out. We weren't quite ready to make peace.

"Yes, but you broke the red violin."

"*That* was an accident."

"Tell that to Freud."

"Sure, water under the bridge, a long time ago now. I am almost twenty-two years old, with a bright future bound to unfold. According to Shane."

"Oh, well then, Shane should know."

Shane ~
Sea Shacking & Relaxing

I liked living in Logan's basement. It was comfortable. Everything I needed was there and Logan could pretend to be looking after me, too. Some people forget, but Logan was with me when we found Banerjee and Harpreet. I know Logan hasn't shaken it off yet because he still talks about Banny *dangling*. He calls her Banny now. Almost making like he knows her. Sometimes when I close my eyes that's what I see—Banny dangling.

Don't know what the fuck happened at the Arbutus Pub on Point Grey Road. I know likely I was a bit too wasted for the public's consumption. Gotta quit beer for breakfast, wake and bake with weed won't work anymore. I was doing fine until some asshole was saying something stupid about immigrants. I nicely told him to stop; he didn't, so he got punched in the face. Then his friend got punched in the face. But, I'll tell ya, sure as shit, soon as the cops arrived I quit punching, anyone and fucking everyone. I had promised no more punching cops, never, ever. Sorry, Nina.

My parents got killed in a car accident when Nina and I were eighteen. Nina took it real hard. She cried and cried and cried some more. It was just fucking terrible. I mean the folks were gone, but Nina was just fucked over badly about the news. She couldn't stop crying.

After I busted up the Arbutus pub, and it really was not that big of a deal, really, and just before we took our seats in court, Nina said I had to live with her as part of my plea bargained *agreed* probation conditions. Had to move out of Logan's place, and even though he is just like a brother to me, judge said, "Nina's place or jail, your choice."

I was just about to tell the judge my choice when Ned's mum put her hand on my shoulder, stood up and said, "Thank you, your Honour, Mr. Bighill's choice is on crown counsel's record, as you may see filed on the form in front of you." And that was that. We all trotted out of court, got in our respective cars, and drove away.

As long as Wendy was with Logan she got a pass with me—she's with Logan, get it? I know she didn't like me. Maybe it's my red hair. She's blonde and they can be difficult.

Ned says, "Two to tango and two sides to a story."

Ned's gonna be an anthropologist. I *audit* classes with him. And I don't pay the tuition. Archeology and anthropology are different families not twins like Nina and me.

Raj teases Ned, and says, "Anthropologists and Archeologists will argue a thousand years from now when they dig up tanning beds. Dr. So says they were used to fry folks who misbehave as a form of punishment. Dr. Z disagrees noting different cultures do different ceremonies. I say, who knows but the hypothesis blows."

Ned shakes his head, "Raj, its *social* science."

Although Nina made like I could decorate my new bedroom any way I wanted, I just said, "No, its good just the way it is, thanks Nina." Ned helped her put the new bed together. He's good at that stuff, a real helpful guy.

Nina and Ned got back from dinner at the Topanga Café. They brought me take out enchiladas and gave me their leftover doggie bags, too.

"Shane," Ned sat down across from me, "you want to go over to Uncle R's sea-shack for a while and relax?"

I looked over at Nina who was lurking over his shoulder, "Yeah, yeah, I'm coming too." She said with a smile.

And before you know it the sojourn morphed into a good group going. Logan, Raj, Wendy, and even Ned's older sister, Amelia were all coming. Even some talk about seeing if Harpreet could come—it could happen. The sea-shack is semi-wheel chair accessible.

I love going to Uncle R's sea-shack—nothing but good times.

Party On!

Mayne Island Elephant

"Shut up Shane, I'm not squeezing the G-D paddle and don't you dare try to tip my canoe!"

"Kayak, it's a kayak." Shane smiled ear to ear. "Inuit roll!"

Yesterday, I had gone out twice with Shane and Ned in the big double seater kayak and felt confident enough to go out today in one of the singles. Turns out to be way harder that those two goofballs said it would be. "Use your rudder."

Earlier their discussion was Einstein's quote: "A ship is always safe at shore, but that isn't what it is built for." It made me smile. The kayak is a well-designed boat, for sure.

I stopped paddling and floated with the current. Raj, Logan, and Wendy were back at the cottage preparing dinner. I could hear them bickering across the water. Someone should tell them how sound travels across the water. But then again, who wants to tell them anything because they were actually having a tonne of fun. Every now and then Wendy would swat one of them on the bum. Amelia and Harpreet were sitting on the deck doing some sort of computer virtual simulation game. They would both make noises indicating terror, joy or excitement. We could not tell from out here. I had my own issues dealing with splashes.

This was a good idea. I had never been to Mayne Island before. Shane said he'd only been here a dozen times or so with Ned and the gang. He was relaxed, happy and having a good time. "This is our tribe Ninnie," Shane explained, the day we were hiking to the top of Mayne Island's Mount Parke.

Again, we talked about the elephant walking behind us on the trail. "I really don't know if I hurt anyone or not. I got too wasted, drinking and smoking shit. Ninnie, I just don't know. I don't think so, but I don't know." Shane said, with such a hangdog look I couldn't do anything but smile back and say, "Don't worry, we'll sort it out."

Shaking his head, Shane said, "Liar."

Ned ~
Harpreet Can Travel

Getting Harpreet over to Mayne Island was a lot easier than I first thought it would be. It was Shane's idea. "Ned, we gotta take Harry on a field trip, eh? C'mon, you can do it. You got a license. Hey buddy, whats the NIKE slogan?"

This pseudo-modern world is still not as wheelchair accessible as it should be but we got it done. And oh my, my, my, Harpreet was having fun. He can't speak without tech support, but his smile and sounds makes it all worthwhile. Shane too. Harry still cannot walk, but Amelia and Raj are working on it. It could happen, some day soon, I hope.

The Dhaliwals have a minivan equipped to transport Harry and his heavy wheelchair. No one spends more time with Harry than Shane. Of course, Shane has always had more time than the rest of us. Shane always had blocks of time where he was either kicked out of school, fired from whatever job he was trying to hold down, or whatever. Shane has time on his side. Mrs. Dhaliwal let Shane use their minivan to take Harry on fieldtrips. Shane has lost his driver's license a couple times. Who knows, but maybe he shouldn't drive. Nowadays, Shane takes Harry all over the city using buses and sky-trains with wheelchair access. They are the best of friends. They both got ankle-bite tattoos.

I was eleven when we first met Harpreet. Now eleven years have flown by since then. Although unlike Raj and Amelia, my mathematical skills are straightforward. I would think that eleven plus eleven would equal a one hundred percent increase, as we are currently age twenty-two. Raj and Amelia argue, count and debate differently. I've learned not to get involved. Both are too smart for me to deal with when I'm not prepared. Number people.

"Raj, Raj, Raj, you are missing the big picture! Remember, Einstein had a sign in his Princeton office that read: *Not everything that counts can be counted and not everything that is counted counts.*"

None of us knew anything about cerebral hypoxia until we met Harpreet. Specifically, Harpreet has hypoxic ischemic encephalopathy. His brain was deprived of oxygen, but it was not a total or fatal deprivation. His heart kept beating in conjunction with our cardiopulmonary resuscitation enough to keep him alive.

Once he got to the hospital they connected life support machines and put him into a medically induced coma. Back then they said Harry had irreversible brain damage. Currently, Amelia and Raj hypothesize differently and believe brain recovery is possible. Amelia has been working with nanobots for years. Raj does software/hardware artificial intelligence development. They bicker all the time. Nina now has some involvement. Nina never bickers; she listens and thinks for a while before speaking.

Amelia has always been in a hurry—*fire, aim, ready.*

Shane Says: Forgive to Live

"Fucking Malik family and their workers called the cops on Harry and me!"

Nina, near tears, said, "Yes, Shane, I got a call, too."

I had to jump in to help move the convo to a calm safe shore. "Shit, Shane," I held both hands up with peace symbols, "your *forgive to live* campaign is honourable, but you have to remember Banerjee's family has always resisted any of our offers and suggestions. They may never be ready to forgive and that's just how they are going to live. We have to leave them alone.

"Wasn't doing it for those fuckers," Shane scowled, "was doing it for Harry."

Evidently, Shane's soft approach of letters and emails to the Malik family failed to get the desired result, so he and Harpreet showed up at their house under the auspices of *forgive to live*.

For the umpteenth time my phone rang. "Ned, did that asshole Shane get Harry in trouble with the cops?" Logan asked with an accelerated level of anger.

"Nothing is simple, Logan," I sighed, "gotta call you back later."

Nina was crying.

Lots of stress these days. We are all a little emo from time to time.

Old Files Are Now New

These days I seldom take a new file, yet sometimes an old file leads to a new one. Of course, I can't abandon my previous patients. After all they are the historical ones who got me to this point—one file at a time.

Cheryl Baines, a lawyer who knew me through a connection with Harjit first referred Paula Farrow to me in the fall of 1997. At that time she was seven years old, in the second grade. Paula would recite the alphabet backwards rather than the forward method her teacher preferred. She started storybooks from the back to front. When asked, Paula simply said, "I like working bottom to top. I know most people are top to bottom people, but I'm not. Its just the way I am."

As a favour to Harjit, I took the case. Thought about referring the file to my friend Lise Donnelly, an accomplished school psychologist, but everyone fixated on me taking her on my caseload. "She needs an experienced applied cognitive psychologist."

I saw Paula a half dozen times, met with her parents, her teachers, brother, grandmother, and decided I had enough to write a report. Really there was nothing wrong with Paula, but I was no longer offering the GORK (God Only Really Knows what is wrong) diagnosis. Simply decided to say she shows some Oppositional Defiant Disorder tendencies. The IQ tests say she has intelligence in the Superior range, no learning disabilities, and she has anxiety. "It remains important to monitor Paula's progress and please call if I might be of any additional assistance."

So, of course, when I got the message saying Paula needs an updated diagnosis for college admission accommodations I smiled, thinking about backwards alphabet recitations.

"Hi Dr. Reilly, this is Paula Farrow calling. Don't know if you remember me or not. You saw me when I was a little kid. Anyhow, James, the counselling advisor, says I need an *updated* assessment. Something about x-rays get dated and test scores do too. He said you'd understand what he meant. It's all the same to me. I have the same number. Thanks."

My colleague, Bruno Zamburn, can't cope with voicemail. If you call him, the greeting message is: "Hello, thanks for calling me. Please send an email."

I did that for a while because my reading decoding and comprehension is superior to voicemail interpretations. Some people prattle on too long and it is hard for me to figure out—what do you want? Reading is easier.

I switched to a traditional voicemail message greeting when too many people took exception to the 'send an email' suggestion. I liked it while it lasted. My sister, Annette, always feels like it is her mission to correct my mistakes. And I always give in to her too easily. Sibling rivalry only goes so far.

I met Paula at the York Street Psychology office. She sat down and said, "Dr. Reilly, it doesn't look like *anything* has changed here in twenty years."

"Well," I smiled, "I'm sure some changes have occurred. Even so stability is always nice, eh?"

"Is this office still set up for deaf people?"

"Sorry?"

"Last time I was here the telephones didn't ring and a light flashed instead."

"Oh, yes, that system is still in place." Paula was and is intrigued by the telephone system Harjit had installed after she had taken on a couple of hearing-impaired clients. In addition to learning sign language, Harjit immersed herself from an ethnographic perspective into the hearing impaired culture. She had the ringers on our office telephones disconnected and a light would flash signaling an incoming call. Deaf people cannot hear the telephone ring. And although it has been an awfully long time since Harjit ever used these offices, I never bothered to get the ringers connected. I liked the flashing light system. Paula did too.

We had three sessions together and I updated Paula's test scores in a report for the college adjudicators.

In our debriefing session Paula asked, "What was the deal with James the counsellor guy saying my test scores were stale? He said you couldn't use old dental records or old test scores."

"Yes, well James is referring to an old validity issue. If a dentist was suggesting a root canal procedure based on dated dental x-rays we would likely ask for new film, and maybe a second opinion. Same with the test scores in the sense that they can become stale."

"Last time you told my parents personality is a stable construct."

Head nodding with a smile, "Yes, that is true, most personality theorists agree personality is stable unless significant trauma occurs. If you hit your head or experience something terrible your personality likely changes or evolves. We haven't seen each other in close to twenty years. You seem much the same personality-wise to me."

Paula flashed me a peace sign, "Yes, makes sense to me. You seem the same too."

We began disengaging and moving to the door. I gave her the usual departure line, "Let me know if there is anything else I can do."

Paula turned looked me in the eye and said, "Well, now that you mention trauma, my brother said he actually saw a couple of guys get killed. That's got to be traumatic, eh? Maybe he could talk to you?"

"Sure, no problem," I held the door open. "Tell him to give me a call."

A new file—opening soon.

The Oxford Comma

—sung by Logan Meyers

The Oxford Comma

An old friend of mine

Comes around to help out

From time to time to time

Is it an Oxford Comma

Separating me from you

Beginnings and endings

A long list of the truths

And I'm losing my youth

Wendy Wendy

Please come home soon

You know I'm in love with you.

Wendy's Moving Back

I like Logan, don't necessarily love him, yet maybe I could. Just can't settle for second best, or something less, but I don't know. He's nice, kind, and awfully loving toward me. He is also contained, always restrained, and he claims to be an internalizer still recovering from juvenile PTSD. And that is his excuse for *everything*.

Our unabated breakup then makeup is getting tiresome. We keep doing it too often. The last time was my fault, most definitely, my bad. We were going for a simple bite to eat with Ned and Nina at Burgoos on Sasamat. Not a big dress up thing, but Logan was wearing white socks and sandals. Guess I may have overreacted and got a little too loud and angry. Why can't he dress a bit more debonair, like Ned?

Another time I may have pushed too hard was when Shane was living in our basement. In the beginning Logan said it was only for a little while until Shane sorted himself out. "Shane will *never* sort himself out. He will always be fucked up! You have to decide—Shane or me?" Logan stammered and hesitated so I packed my stuff and stormed out.

I moved back after Shane had to move out due to a probation order. Logan let Raj move into the basement. No problem, I like Raj. He's a smart scientific sort of a guy, but not too pedantic or anything. We get along just fine. He cleans up after himself.

Recently, we were scheduled to go to Seattle and that is another one that is on me. What happened was, Logan was upstairs in the shower, his cell phone was sitting on the table beside me, and it started to ring. Call display showed the word MOTHER along with a skull and cross bones picture. Of course, I answered. It might have been some family crisis or something. Logan never talks about his mother much. I have met his dad, three times.

I answered, "Hello."

"Hello, who is this?"

"Pardon, who is this? You called me."

"No, I am calling my son's number! Who are you?"

"Okay, your son's name is?" I asked the caller.

"My son's name is Logan Meyers. Who are you?"

I realized perhaps I had overstepped a little and tried to back paddle, "Oh so sorry, my apologies I thought you may have been a telemarketer. Hi, I'm Wendy, Logan's girlfriend."

"Logan has a girlfriend?"

"Yes, we have been together for quite a while now."

"May I speak to Logan, please?"

"Sorry, he's in the shower. And he takes long showers. I will get him to call you when he gets out."

"Yes, please do so," she sighed. "I have a concert coming and it would be wonderful if you and Logan could attend."

His mother plays first violin for the Seattle Symphony Orchestra. "For sure, we'd *love* to come." I said without first checking with Logan. No big deal gone wrong, right.

Logan finally came downstairs and went a little wingy on me. "You answered *my* phone. You spoke with *my* mother. What the fuck were you thinking?"

"I wasn't thinking you'd go all weird on me." I said defensively. "Concert in Seattle, c'mon. It'll be fun."

"You know *nothing*!" He shrieked at me. "My mother and fun do not go together." He grabbed his jacket, waved the cell phone in my face, slammed the door and left.

He came home drunk as a skunk at one in the morning. Woke me up saying stupid stuff like, "If you want to go to Seattle we can. I love you Wendy."

In the end we didn't go to Seattle, we got a better offer. Ned's uncle has a cottage in the Gulf Islands and a group of us were going over to chill out and relax before the next phase of Shane's trial.

Using *my* cell phone I had to call Logan's mother and explain the situation.

"Clearly, Logan and I have a lot of work to do relationship-wise. You know, what they say, Rome wasn't built in a day."

Shit, then she started crying so I had to come up with something, "For sure we will come to Seattle to celebrate Logan's birthday with you. You're his mother and that makes it your birthday too. I promise! I can make this happen. See you soon."

She sniffled and simply said, "Okay."

"Okay, listen, it's the sisterhood, we're good. Trust me, I keep my promises!"

"Tell Logan I love him."

"Me too."

"What?"

"I love him too."

Part Four

Logan ~
Who Were Trent and Declan

"Although Trent McKinney called himself a halfbreed *because he came* from the village of Floydston, which straddles the Saskatchewan and Manitoba border line, he really was just a farmboy who fell in with the wrong crowd." Dr. Dudra leaned back and waited for another question.

Sort of rocking on the spot, Jedd Talbot just stood there in the middle of the courtroom staring at the floor for like what seemed to last forever. Finally, Jedd asked, "And the other lad, what about him?"

"Declan Downes, on the other hand, was a complicated kid. He grew up in a nice upper middleclass family in Kerrisdale. On the *Introvert/Extrovert Scale of Behaviour* Declan's test score falls off the end of the normal curve."

Jedd tilted his head, squinted and asked, "Top or bottom of the scale?"

Dr. Dudra sat upright, "Sorry, forgive me, I should say Declan achieved the highest score I have ever seen."

"And how many test scores have you seen Dr. Dudra?"

"Hundreds."

"Hundreds, you say?"

"Yes, hundreds, I've been practicing in this area for over thirty years."

Wendy was tapping me on the thigh and whispering in my ear, "Logan, whats going on now?"

I tried to give her the eyebrow raise, as if to say: Please not now. It didn't work and I had to whisper in her ear, "Please, we can't talk right now."

And of course, in turn, Raj pokes me and shakes his head with disapproval.

Good thing we got seats in row three.

Amelia's Legal Mind

"The electric light did not come from the continuous improvement of candles." *~Author Unknown*

❧

Evidently my sister has a brilliant legal mind, according to the famous lead lawyer, Jedd Talbot. And my mum capitulates to anything Jedd says. So, seated at the defendant's table we have Jedd as first chair, Amelia sits second, and my mum comes in at the end third place. But everyone knows who she is. Even the mayor is here to show her support.

A couple days ago mum and I were having a nice bite of lunch when I casually mentioned, "Shane says he doesn't really know, he might have done it. You know his history. Remember when he busted up the Arbutus Pub."

Dramatically, she looked up at me, dropped her fork, and I knew a storm was brewing. If Amelia was with us she'd say, "Pass the butane mum's going to light her hair on fire."

Rather, she collected herself quickly, and softly said, "At this point and until the whole process has run its course I want you to remember, Shane is *innocent* until the Crown Prosecutors convince the jury that he is guilty beyond a reasonable doubt."

Anthropologically speaking, I do not understand too much about the Canadian criminal justice system. Wasn't interested until now. My girlfriend Nina is even worse. She is strictly a scientist and scrutinizes social sciences saying they are rigged with bias, methodologically flawed, and lack replication. These things are easier for me.

When we were kids mum monitored and regulated how much, and what type of traditional television Amelia and I could watch. Of course, Amelia quickly figured out how to defeat the parental control parametres. Mum was none the wiser, so Amelia and I watched all sorts of American crime lab, courtroom dramas, and blood and guts type series. It was great. Too bad it was mostly phony bologna. Had a great childhood, even the Byng thing wasn't that bad for me. Sure screwed up Shane and Logan. Raj was with me when it happened and he seems solid. Don't think the Byng thing messed up Raj, but I don't really know.

We all have issues.

Wendy ~
You Had One Job

Just when Logan and I were doing so well back together, again, I got sucked into Shane's shenanigans. Raj and Logan were planning to drive to Seattle to pick up hardware parts for Harpreet's equipment. "These kind of specialized microprocessors and bots are usually available in the States but way too expensive in Canada," Raj explained, with such excitement it was almost contagious. "India is too far away to travel, but we could if we had to. I have a friend in Delhi with connections."

These days shipping some stuff across the border are difficult so we used Logan's mother's address in Seattle. She was happy to help and they were all scheduled for lunch *together*. I helped facilitate the rendezvous. A clear win-win situation and everyone was happy. Everybody loves Raj.

Court proceedings were in a one week recess while Judge Wallace attended to some prearranged family matters. One of the boys was supposed to take Shane downtown for a meeting with Jedd Talbot. "Last time, Shane skipped a Talbot meeting and slept the day away with a hangover," Logan explained with a very serious look on his face. "That did not go down well with anyone."

"Hey, no problem, I can take him," I declared. Shane and I were getting along really well now that he lives with his sister Nina.

"You can, you will?" Logan seemed so pleased. "Thanks, Wendy, that's a big help. We can't have Shane missing meetings at this stage in the game."

All those guys do sports analogies, mantras and stupid stuff. I never understand half of it; even so, I go along and say, "Yeah, no kidding, no screw-ups this late in the game. I got this one!"

Logan called Shane. Everything was set up, confirmed and ready to go. Shane would be expecting me to pick him up tomorrow at ten in the morning. A right reasonable time of day—not too early and not so late that it takes the good part of the day away. If you know what I mean. Logan didn't, but no matter, it was a commitment I could handle.

I had *one job*, so of course I knew to get there early. Logan warned me that Shane's sister Nina leaves for the lab really early and there was a strong likelihood that Shane might be sleeping later than he should. "Call before you leave and make sure he is awake and getting ready to go," Logan recommended.

So I called Shane's cell number, got no response, no voicemail, nothing. I called their house's landline—Nina, Logan, and who knows who like landlines. "Why would you need a landline *and* a cell phone," I asked, only to get a convoluted answer. Seems like a waste of money to me. Don't talk to Logan about wasting money because that convo is a waste of time!

Ringing the bell, knocking on the door, and then subsequently pounding on the door produced nothing. I had one job, but now concern was coming over me. I called Logan's cell number. He has a fancy car from his father, which rings through the stereo. He answers straight away asking, "Trouble with Shane?"

"Yes," I explained. "I called Shane before leaving our place, now I'm here ringing the bell and pounding on the door, but nothing's happening. And Logan, their neighbours are looking my way, too."

Raj pipes in from the passenger seat, "Wendy, see the flower pots on the front porch stoop?"

"Yes."

"Under the third one is a key."

"These flower things are big. I can't pick it up."

"You don't have to pick it up, just *tilt* it."

"Okay, got it. I got the key and I'm going inside." I waved to the neighbours followed with a thumb up sign to let them know I am cool. Thinking to myself, please don't call the cops.

"Are you in?" Raj asked.

"Yes, what should I do now?"

"Start calling out his name," Logan yelled at me.

I could tell Raj poked him, whispering, and "Don't yell at her."

"Shane, it's Wendy! SHANE IT'S WENDY. I'm not getting anything here guys."

"That's okay, Shane sleeps in the basement. You are going to have to go down there and check on him," Raj says in a soft cajoling voice that was hard to say no to, yet I did not want to go downstairs. Of course, Shane likes basements. He is a basement kinda guy.

Slowly proceeding down the stairs, clutching my cell phone and calling out, "Shane, its me, Wendy. Shane, are you here? Its me Wendy." No response from Shane. "Sorry Logan, dunno, but there is no good way to tell you this. Sometimes I'm scared with Shane. And its not just because he's accused of killing those people."

Raj jumped in, "Just stay cool Wendy. Sometimes he sleeps with headphones on. Just check it out."

Sure enough, there he was lying in his bed with headphones over his ears. "He's here!" I shouted. "You were right Raj, he's got headphones on."

"Wake him up!" Logan yelled at me.

I could hear Raj whispering in the background, "Don't yell at her. It doesn't help."

"Shane, SHANE, WAKE UP!" and I poked him, knocked off the headset, moving backwards quickly.

Slowly, very slowly, it seemed to me, Shane regained consciousness. Raj and Logan were screaming at him through my cell phone. "GET OUT OF BED SHANE! PITTER, PATTER, YOU GOTTA GET AT 'ER!"

Shane started to smile, "What's up Wendy, what you doing here?"

I passed him the phone, "What's up Logan?"

Logan snorted, "Shane you are going downtown with Wendy. You gotta meet with JT."

Nodding his head, Shane said, "Oh yeah, right, you are Mr. Super Star."

Raj joined in, "Shane, it's Raj here buddy, you okay?"

"Yeah, yeah, I'm fine Raj. Just slept in is all. We're cool, I'll be ready to go in ten." Shane passed me the phone.

"Okay guys we're good here time-wise. See you later alligator."

"In a while crocodile," Logan responded. I felt relieved he was responding favourably with a familiar chant.

Raj signed off with, "Thanks Wendy, we owe you big time."

I made some hand gestures Shane's way to indicate I'd be waiting upstairs.

He nodded, gave me a thumbs up sign, and said, "How much time I really got?"

"Oh, geez, we're cool," I assured Shane. "I think half hour or so, you know."

"No, I don't know that's why I'm asking you."

"Push off in twenty, half hour, I dunno, it's your show."

"Okay," he got out of bed. Shane sleeps naked.

I went upstairs, sat down at the kitchen table and waited. Thank goodness, this event was starting to look like it was going to work out just fine. And then I thought: Don't jinx it, we are not there yet. Logan always says "Close, but no cigar." I know that must mean something and sometime I'll Google it and find out. It was too quiet downstairs.

I just kept thinking—You had one job.

Do not screw this up.

Shane & Wendy Wake & Bake

For the longest time I didn't like Wendy very much, didn't think she was good for Logan. She's so controlling, judgmental and criticizes everything. She makes Logan wear clothes her way saying his way's nerdy. Whatever, I don't care anymore and it doesn't matter anyway because Logan really, really wanted a girlfriend. And the blonde business was what he was all about. I thought she might be a fake blonde, but no way would I say so to Logan. He thinks she's the real deal. Infatuated, enamoured, I don't know, Wendy's with Logan and that's all that matters. She gets a pass.

I really liked living in Logan's basement. It's comfortable, everything I needed was there. Then the court's judge said I was on probation and had to live with Nina. Didn't want to do that at first, and then Nina gets all mushy about me being her twin and the only family she has left. Then she says sometimes she gets scared at night and wouldn't be so much so if I was with her for a while. "Just stay with me for a while until I get over this feeling of loneliness. Our parents are gone Shane. I still feel bad about that and I'm going to need you to keep eyes on me for a little while. Okay?"

"Ok!" Nina needs me. "Yeah, sure, I can hang with you a while."

Should say, as long as Wendy is *nice* to Logan she gets a pass with me. She moved in with us and then she moved out. Now there's talk she's coming back, again. Whenever she was gone Logan got blubbery about missing her. She'd come back and he'd be all smiles and the old Logan again. So she gets a pass with me - as long as she's nice to Logan.

Logan's my *under-the-stall-pal*. We'd just become teenagers. We're looking forward to getting older so people wouldn't treat us like little kids anymore. Thought that once we were teenagers everything would be okay. Logan's thirteenth birthday party was a big thing. His dad went all crazy on the party. Their old house was up for sale and Mr. Meyers was gonna have a big party for Logan.

Grade eight wasn't so great, either. Sometimes I just got sorta sad and would lock myself in the school's bathroom stall in between French and math classes. Logan would crawl under the stall and explain that I must come out soon so as not to get in trouble. Logan hates getting in trouble. It's never bothered me the way it gets to Logan. He'd always say stuff like, "Don't draw attention to us. Its not a good thing."

Things were not so good at home neither. My parents were losing patience with me and told me so all the time. And Nina would get angry with me whenever she caught me talking to Banny. She'd burst into my bedroom and ask, "What are you doing?"

I'd explain that in my mind I just pictured Banny was sitting in the corner chair and I talked to her. Yes, I know she's not *really* there. I just wanted to talk to her that's all.

❧

All of a sudden Wendy starts shouting at me from the upstairs doorway, "Shane, what are you doing? You're getting ready, right?"

Uh oh, what will I do about Wendy-O? Decided I should just go with the truth and tell her my JT strategy. "Yes, I'm dressed and getting ready. May I please show you something?"

She slowly starts down the stairs, "What would you like to show me?"

"Well, you know," I held up my hands, "I got some issues."

"Don't worry Shane, we all have issues."

"I get what are called *intrusive thoughts.* Ned says just to tell them to fuck off and go away. I also got some anxiety things, too. Used to take a bunch of pills, capsules and stuff. Nina got me this vape machine and that's what I want to show you."

"Okay."

"I keep the vapourizer in the back room here." Opening the door to the vape room, I said, "After you Madame."

"Oh, so, this is your den of iniquity?"

Smiling back, I said, "Something like that. Here, have a seat." She sat down and I started assembling a bowl for the vape machine. All the while explaining how my anxiety issues work. "Haven't had a full fledged panic attack for a while, but I got some other issues."

"Yes, well I have issues too," Wendy sighed.

"Mr. JT makes me nervous." I plugged the vapourizer in to warm up.

"How come he makes you nervous?"

"Dunno guess maybe cuz Ned's mom is always going gaga about Mr. JT. She says *we* are really lucky to have him on our team. He's smart and stuff. For the longest time she was my lawyer. Now she's saying she's over her head with the new charges and he's gonna be a big help."

Wendy smiled and said, "Know your limit and stay within it."

"Yeah, something like that."

"Complicated process, eh?"

"Yeah, I usually don't know what's going on. Sometimes I have to go to court and other times they appear for me and I stay at home. Then there's the arraignment, pleas, bail and a bunch of other stuff that makes no sense to me. Today I gotta go talk to Mr. JT about disclosure rules." I stirred the weed in the vape bowl.

Wendy scrunched up her face and asked, "What are you doing?"

"Nina says smoking joints stinks up the house and this machine is better. You know there are only two types of flames for combustion. The gaseous flame and this type, which is a pyrolyzing burn. You can't smell the weed burning cuz it is vapourized." I passed the nozzle end to Wendy, "Want the first hit?"

"What?" she scrunched her face even more this time? Now, in the morning?"

"Wake and bake. I always smoke some weed in the morning, especially if I have to go see Mr. JT. It takes away some of my anxiety and the tension."

"Wake and bake?" Wendy was wondering how it works and took a good hit. "What the hell—when in Rome," she said passing to me.

I took a toke and passed back to Wendy, who was coughing a bit. "Careful, this weed is smooth, with a kicker."

"Really smooth!" she waved her hands in the air.

The first bowl went quickly and I started to prepare another when Wendy went wingy, "No more, no more, no mas!"

"No mas?" I asked.

"Yes, that is Spanish for *no more!* Oh geez Biggy, we're way too wasted. I fucked up!"

She's calling me Biggy now, "What do you mean, you fucked up?"

"I HAD ONE JOB TODAY AND I FUCKED IT UP!"

"What, we're cool, there's no problems here." I tried to calm her down.

"I can't tell Logan we waked and baked, smoked weed, and missed the meeting with Jedd Talbot!"

"We haven't missed the meeting. Its not until ten," I explained.

"It's 9:45."

"We got plenty of time."

"No we don't. I'm wasted. I can't drive. You can't drive. You lost your license!"

"Hey, hey, hey, driving is for dummies. We'll take bikes. You can use one of Nina's bikes. Shes got a few to choose from."

"Bikes?"

"Yeah, yeah, parking's not a problem with the bikes."

"We can't get there in fifteen minutes." She looked close to tears.

"No worries, we'll be close if we leave now," I explained. "Besides, Mr. JT *always* runs late. Ned was with me last time and he says just stay cool. JT runs late and it doesn't mean anything. Lets get going!"

Turns out, Wendy's actually kinda cool. I like her. Didn't know about her issues, until today.

We all got issues.

Jedd ~

Cancer, Threats, and the Rest

"Remember, after the game has been played the King and Pawn are both placed in the same box." ~Allen H. Soroka, LLB, MLS.

***

The cancer treatments were becoming more complicated than what they first advertised to me, "You know we will sue for false advertising." Joking was a better defensive mechanism a while back. The treatment time took was longer than predicted, too.

"Sorry Mr. Talbot, we are doing our best for you."

"Right."

This kid Shane's case was supposed to be open and shut. It's taking more time than I thought, but I don't mind. Shane's a good kid. Besides, said I'd do it and now I'm doing it and too many other things, concurrently. Life gets that way sometimes for a while before settling to a copeable rhythm. I usually cope well.

"Nurse, nurse," I called over with my most cajoling voice. I couldn't go any further today, this just isn't working out very well, and I've got to get out of here.

She could see me waving, heard me call, but was busy, planning to get to me as a matter of course, or in turn in good time. I've been here so many times now I know how the Cancer Centre works. All of a sudden from out of nowhere the beautiful, nicest nurse of all times appeared and was slowly strolling down the hall. I knew she would help me.

"Hi, hello, bonjour," I caught her eye.

The nice nurse's smile makes me feel at ease every time. "Yes," she came towards me asking, "How is Mr. Talbot today?"

"Great, fine, fine, thanks," I started to explain. "I need you to help me out this morning."

Reassuringly, she touched my hand, "Of course, what can I do for you?"

"I need you to disconnect me from the equipment because I am unable to stay today. I have to get over to my office immediately."

"Oh dear that sounds awfully important, but I'm afraid I can't do that," she said smiling the whole time.

"Of course you can," I implored her. "I have a kid charged with murder waiting for me at my office. You have to let me out of here."

"Awfully sorry Mr. Talbot, he's going to have to wait a while longer until your treatment is over today." Then she walked away!

The nasty nurse, still scowling, shook her head, and walked over towards me. "I know who you are and what you do for a living. Saw you on the television talking about that kid. My kid went to school with him. She says no way would he kill anyone." She started disconnecting me from the chemo cancer equipment. "You better not rat me out for helping you leave too early."

"Never," I said with a nodding head. "No rats here," I assured her.

"But, you have to call Dr. Donnelly and reschedule."

"Yes, yes, I'll call Toby right away to reschedule."

"Promise."

"Yes, I promise, my assistant will do it today."

"Your *assistant?*"

"Believe me, she's the best ever, really. The best." With my free arm I pulled out my cell phone and spoke into it. "Angela, please call Dr. Toby Donnelly and reschedule today's treatment. Also, could you please let Shane Bighill know I'm running late. He is scheduled at ten."

The nurse waved a one-handed flapping goodbye as I hightailed it out of the treatment room.

"Thanks." I think we both knew I'm done with this shit for a while. It's just not working out for me. I've got things to do.

Cancer can wait.

Wendy ~
Carnivals & Their Cigars

"If I had eight hours to chop down a tree, I'd spend the first six sharpening my axe." ~Abe Lincoln

Must admit I did not like Shane when I first met him. And it's not the Irish ideology or anything, more like my *own* narrowness. Yes, I'm working on that, too. Our friendship had a head on collision the day I took him downtown to meet with the fearless legal leader, Mr. Jeddsterman. Now some folks say Shane and are inseparable. Harpreet had a role in that part. Logan likes it now that Shane and I are good friends.

Logan says, "So glad you two are friends! Something I wanted all along."

We started poorly. On my big day debut, for some reason Shane convinced me that smoking pot prior to meeting with the lawyer was a good idea. "Go along to get along," my mother's motto. And the only people who fail are those that do not try. I never knew much about anxiety until Shane's explanation made it all crystal clear. Smoking weed seemed to help him—not me. I started to freak out. I had one job and that was to get Shane downtown to the lawyer's office.

It was powerful pot and I was panicking because I'd promised Logan, "No problem, I'll get Shane to his lawyer's appointment, *on time.*"

Additionally, the task required a type of interpreter to accompany Shane. His hearing was adequate, while listening was another matter altogether. Hence, someone from our crew always went along to listen and subsequently explain, re-frame, and clarify the facts/fiction over a beer. I preferred coffee.

At any rate, my turn at taking Shane downtown to Jeddman's office started off poorly. First, I had to get him out of bed. He was sound asleep when I arrived. After smoking pot, no way could I drive downtown. Yet Shane convinced me of the efficacy of riding one of his sister's many bicycles.

"Here, this road bike will fit you," he said, while strapping an orange helmet on my head.

"Okay, lets go!"

Nothing but a smile with some screams of glee from both him and me, the bike ride was better than driving. It was faster too! Maybe a bit too fast in a couple places due to my central nervous system's malfunctioning. Both my mind and brain reacted to the marijuana. Shane was the fearless leader—for today.

"This is great Wendy," Shane said as we were pedaling down the bike path. "You know, the people you never get to know because no time, different stripes and stuff. This is great, I get to know you."

I gulped, choked, and struggled back a watery eye. "Yes, you got it buddy, I am so glad I know you, too. Logan was right."

"Logan?"

"Yeah, he says you're the champ, his best friend ever!"

"Ah, Logan's an idiot, don't listen to him." Shane saluted. "Down hill coming, no brakes needed." Shane whizzed by with a big smile and hoot.

"Bingo-Bango!"

"Wah who," I screamed too. Normally, going so fast scares me, but not today.

We arrived at 10:10. "See, what'd I tell you about biking," Shane said with a big grin.

"Okay, close but no cigar," I reminded him. "We are not there yet. What floor?"

"Forty-fifth."

"Skyscrapers, let's go." We locked the bikes elaborately, and dashed for the elevators.

Everyone was well dressed and the elevator filled quickly. "Shane, did you push forty-five."

"Oui, Mademoiselle, for you, it is done."

The elevator soared upwards. Stopped a few times before the ding sounded to indicate the forty-fifth floor. We quickly spilled out into the reception area. A large golden jazzy sign greeted us: Talbot and Associates. This place even smelled classy, expensive and golden. There's no such thing as scented air-conditioning, is there?

"Namaste Nicole," Shane greeted the receptionist.

She smiled, "Hello Shane, I'll buzz Mr. Talbot's assistant."

"Thanks Nicole, you're the best."

A moment later an attractive, well-tailored woman arrived. "Good morning Shane," she said softly. "Mr. Talbot is running a little behind schedule. He will be with you shortly. Please come and have a seat in the conference room. May I get you anything?"

"Yes please, two of your fab double espressos would be wonderful. Angela, this is my friend Wendy."

She extended her hand, "Good morning Wendy, pleasure to meet you."

Thought it was cool Shane introducing me as his friend. Didn't think he liked me much.

Angela escorted us down the hall to the conference room. "Ms. Amelia Reilly is here and Ms. Annette is enroute."

"Enroute, eh," Shane said with a note of sarcasm.

"Yes, that is correct, heavy traffic," Angela replied as she opened the double doors to the conference room.

Amelia was sitting at the far end of the table. She had two laptop computers open, a pile of books, and papers scattered in front of her. "Hey Amelia," Shane said, waving his hands as we entered the ornate conference room. "Whatcha doing here, thought you'd be at UBC during the court recess?"

"Nina is in charge at UBC while I am here sitting *second chair for you*," Amelia said with a certain level of authority. And then she winked at me. "Why is everyone always late?"

"Heavy traffic," Shane replied. "You remember Logan's girlfriend Wendy?"

"Of course, we met at the Mayne Island Sea Shack." Amelia got up and came over to give me a greeting hug. "Thanks for making sure Shane got here on time today."

"Hey, hey, hey," Shane said, "don't try and pin that on Wendy. It's my fault."

"I know," Amelia grinned, "Raj called from South Seattle a little while ago. They got the software keys, mircro-copressors, and now they're going somewhere else on Mercer Island to get the VR-Nano-bots."

"VR-Nanobots?"

"Yes, this engineer in South Seattle has developed Virtual Reality Nanobots and is selling them for a semi-reasonable price. Harpreet will freak out when we install them into the new CPU machine."

"Is freaking out a good thing?" I asked.

Shane slugged my shoulder, "Fucking-A, Raj said he could do it, but I thought it was just bullshit."

"No, he's close, and we have some work left, but close." Amelia responded.

"No cigar?" I asked.

Shane thought it was funny and was about to put in his two cents when the double doors burst open. Ms. Reilly, Sr. and the Jeddster came flying in and the room's temperature dropped drastically. "Good morning everyone, sorry I am late," Jeddy said. "Shall we get started? Everyone please take a seat."

Amelia already had her seat selected. I didn't know the pecking order so just followed Shane's lead and sat beside him in the plush leather rolling chair.

Obviously this is Jedder's show, first-chair and all. He looked over at me, "And you are?"

Amelia jumped in, "Yes, Jedd, let me introduce you to Wendy Orton, Shane's friend. Wendy was kind enough to accompany Shane here this morning. And, we've been here a while waiting for you two."

"Again, my apologies for being late. Won't happen again." Just then assistant Angela came through the double doors, handed Jeddsy some paper and files. "Wendy, will you be staying on with us during our meeting?"

Shane looked my way and nodded, so I simply said, "Yes."

"Very well, then," he pulled out some paper, and Angela brought it to my side of the table. "Annette and I hold lawyer/client confidentiality privilege with Shane, but you do not. Therefore we will need you to sign this standard nondisclosure confidentiality agreement so we may speak freely in this room. As is it should go without saying— what is discussed in this room stays in this room."

Shane leaned over whispering, "Its cool, they had Ned sign one too. He calls it legal-ease."

I signed; Angie smiled and placed it in a file folder.

Ms. Reilly Sr. snapped open a book and said, "Okay, great, glad we can all get together today. I'd like to start first by reminding you, Shane, do not talk to *anyone* about your case—no one."

"You've told me that a hundred times," Shane jeered back at her.

"Fine, but I cannot remind you too often. Do not talk to the police, crown attorneys, Dr. Lisa Rae, friends or anyone about what we are doing."

"What are we doing?" Shane asked sarcastically.

Amelia jumped in, "We're trying to keep your ass out of jail. That's what we are doing here."

Jeddism took charge, "Okay, okay, point made Amelia. Let's move along onto other issues. Now Shane, through the legal discovery process where the Crown Prosecutors are required to pass documents for defence examination, we have received Dr. Lisa Rae's Pre-Trial Assessment Report. And for the most part it looks fine to me. Anyone have comments?"

Geez, J-man, of course, the two Reillys' got comments. That's their thing, commenting. Turn taking is not a strong suit, however. This went on for like ever. I forgot I was supposed to be paying attention and report back to Logan. That is, confidentiality forms, legalease, and what not, notwithstanding clauses. The coffee was wiring me too tight too. Why did Shane order double espressos?

"Evidence," Amelia raised her voice and I snapped out of wherever my mind had wandered and was paying attention, again. Who knew about Shane? I'm sure he was zoned out. "Their evidence is circumstantial and those witnesses are weak."

Ms. Reilly Sr. took a deep breath and I sensed it was going to be her turn again. I've learned how this round-the-table stuff works. "Yes, Amelia, these are things we have been over before." She looked over to JTer, "Anything else, my two hours are long over."

Me too, I thought to myself, but no way would I say so. Wow can't believe nobody had to get up and pee for over two hours. Are these people camels or what? And, of course, now that the thought has entered my mind, I have to pee, badly.

Jedderdieah in charge was going to get in the final words, "Yes, okay, good meeting, thanks everyone. So Shane, just a final reminder, now I know you told Ned you do not know whether you committed the act or not. Ned does not know, you do not know, I do not know, none of that matters now. Okay, got it. That is not our issue. The prosecutors must *prove* to a jury, beyond a reasonable doubt that you did do it. That is their job. Monday morning we will be back in court. Let's see what they've got."

And that was it, meeting over. Assistant Angela was the first to stand and start collecting, tidying, and I whispered to Shane, "Gotta pee badly." He pointed the direction and I bolted out to seek relief.

"Excuse me," I shuffled my way out of the conference room and down the hall to a fancy unisex washroom (I think). "Ohhhh," I sighed, perhaps a little louder than need be, but I really had to pee.

"You okay over there Wendy?" Amelia had slid into the washroom.

"Yes, sorry, was I too loud?" I didn't really care, yet she was the real awesome-Amelia, and I was showing respect. Really, she is awesome.

We stood at the sink hand washing, primping, and hair adjusting. "Thanks for bringing Shane this morning. I know he can be challenging. We appreciate the help." Amelia said with such a sincere tone.

I just thought to myself, oh geez, if you only knew, but I said, "No problem."

"On Monday, I want Shane alert in court. Nina and Ned are scheduled to bring him. So, no wake and bake. It's an important appearance. Today was cool, and he did just fine. Thanks again." She patted me on the shoulder. "I gotta get out of here." And she took off.

I re-washed my hands and thought: Amelia knew we were wasted. Shane was waiting for me outside. "Let's go for lunch. I'm famished."

We spent the rest of the day biking around downtown. Nina's bike had a thousand gears and rode like a breeze. We went around Stanley Park, through some trails, back over the Burrard Bridge, and back to Nina's before it got dark. It was a tonne of fun. Shane had me laughing to tears too many times to count.

"So you know the cigar thing. Back when smoking them was cool, the carnival barkers had this sledgehammer-smashing thing. You hit it as hard as you could and if it went to the top it would ring a bell. You got a cigar for ringing the bell. That's where close but no cigar comes from."

"We gotta go to the carnival."

"Yeah, for sure, if I'm not back in jail when it opens, we gotta go."

"Shit Shane!" I spit accidently, "we just spent half a day with your crackerjack legal team. You're *not* going to jail."

"Logan says life is not always a fairytale with a happy ending."

"Aw, Logan, I love him, but he does not know everything!"

"Yeah, Logan's an idiot," Shane said with a smile.

"Bingo-Bango!"

Raj Gill ~ Who Was OJ?

"Always drink upstream from the herd." ~Will Rogers

❦

Can't tell anyone, especially my father, but I miss India. I was doing well and we were doing innovative research at the University of Chandigarh. When my sister called to tell me about Shane, of course, I had to come home. I don't have a bio-brother, so I don't know about the genogram. Yet Shane is like my brother, my friend, compadre, pal, yaar, dosth, Mon ami, and I love him. He's Shane. We've been through a lot together and "it ain't over yet."

I'll go back to India, when the time is right, whenever that might be, but we've got to see Shane through this legal quagmire. No one wants to talk about what if this whole thing goes south. What if Shane did it? He says he doesn't know if he did it or not because he gets uber-wasted with memory blackouts. It's been bothering me ever since I first heard. However, not a word, no negativity; reasonable doubt is what they all talk about. Who was OJ? They always talk about him. Evidently, he got off.

I first met Ned, Logan, and Shane in elementary school. We've always been the best of friends. Every finger on my hand is different and it is the same thing with my friends. Shane's always been a bit eccentric, but wow, was he ever the best foursquare player to come out of Kitsilano Elementary School. A true athlete.

Logan has always been uptight. His brother died when Logan was a little kid, his parents divorced, remarried and divorced again. Logan's been through a lot of social feces. He has a new girlfriend and she seems nice. He loves her, a lot more than I'd expect from him. Whatever, he's Logan, always has been, always will be that way. So we roll with it.

Ned, he's the glue that holds us together, makes us a strong unit. He's the leader, he's the best. Ned always knows the right thing to do.

Yesterday, Logan and I were driving to Seattle. We had some software key cards and a couple of mircro-copressors shipped to his mother's house. Shipping stuff across the border has become difficult, but just showing the border guard what we bought is not.

Logan's mother was awfully happy to see us. I've known her for years; don't remember her being so mushy. Makes my mum seem benign and she is off the Richter scale mushy. Disengaging was difficult. She wanted us to stay overnight. Logan wanted to leave two minutes after arriving. I had to mediate. Parental issues at this age are so awkward. I should know, Pops and I still aren't talking. He's still angry that I left India to attend Shane's trial.

Logan drives an expensive Tesla loaded with all available accessories and gadgets galore. His father buys Logan's affection. Yet their issues are even shallower than I can understand. The car is a dream to drive. Phone calls and facetime stream through the dashboard screen with such clarity it is unbelievable. Wendy called a couple of times because of problems with Shane. Amelia called a half dozen times to make sure we were buying the correct list of software, and hardware items. She had written on a piece of paper, texted, e-mailed, and dictated what we were supposed to say to the digital artificial intelligence engineer on Mercer Island.

"You seem to be getting pretty tight with Professor Amelia," Logan said with an unnecessary shoulder nudge.

"What?" I snickered back. "We're working together, that's all. It's for Harpreet. We're scientists, its applied research."

"Yeah, I knew that, but it's your starry gaze into her eyes that gives it away. The leaning into her and lingering nuzzles make it obvious."

"You're an idiot."

"No, no, you always take things the wrong way," he said waving his hand in the air. "I've always thought Amelia is the prettiest pumpkin in the patch."

"Ah, naw, I'm a little league bunter and she's Triple A all the way. I'm nowhere near her league."

"Raj, Raj, Raj." Logan loves baseball talk. "You, my man, are a homerun slugger swinging for the fences."

"You're an idiot."

Although it is true, Amelia is awfully beautiful, she's out of my league for sure, no doubt, no way, and I could never, ever think otherwise. Logan's an idiot. Amelia is three years older, ten times smarter and ten degrees ahead of me. Still it has been awesome working with her putting together stuff for Harpreet. "Harry's a cool guy," she'd say, "I think there are a lot of things tech can do to help him out. Shane was the first person to put me onto the project."

"Harry's not a *project*!" I tried to put her in her place, but her smile let me know mine.

I've known Amelia all my life, she's Ned's older sister. When we were little kids Amelia knew everything and we knew nothing. Amelia was the first person that talked tech to me. She's been messing around with nanobots for as long as I can remember. She started buying them when they were really expensive. "Everything is cheaper in India," I explained.

"Quality," she said, "is essential. You get what you pay for."

When I returned to Vancouver for Shane's trial I ended up spending time with Amelia. Part of it was car-pooling to the courthouse, part of it was Ned, and mostly she just seemed interested in what I was doing at U of C. And then out of the blue, she gives me the big invitation. "Raj, you should come up to the lab at UBC. I'll show you around. We're doing some good work. Nina in particular is doing fascinating work with DNA decomp and synthesizing mutant compounds. I could hire you as a research assistant. We've got the funding, but not the talent."

Thought I'd about pee my pants with excitement, "Yes, for sure, I am available."

"Cool." She held out her hand, we shook. "See you tomorrow at nine."

I couldn't believe it. Amelia had her own lab, she's working on medical and law degrees concurrently, and now she's sitting second chair on Shane's trial. To say my infatuation is just an understatement is like saying I've hit the big leagues.

Play ball.

Sunday Sociology & Dinner

A six-person dinner, really, is no big thing. Even so, mother frets about pedestrian details that would never cross my mind. And I'm doing all of the work. She's nervous about tomorrow morning. Seems Jedd is sick or something and cannot make it to dinner. No problem, I parachuted Raj into his spot. The table is set: fancy dishes, and dining paraphernalia, too.

"Did you speak with Jedd today?" she asks, with a type of tone that is not needed.

"No, mum, it's Sunday, most people don't work Sundays."

"Jedd was supposed to come for dinner, but left a cryptic message saying he wasn't feeling well." She looks at me with more intensity than needed.

"Mum, relax." I tapped her on the shoulder. A hug would not help at this point. "We're good to go. Tomorrow will be fine. We are as prepared as can be and ready to go."

"How about Shane?"

"He's with Logan and Wendy and they are doing their thing. I just spoke to him an hour ago."

"What's their thing?"

"Board games! They play stupid board games ad nauseum." I snorted with exasperation.

"Okay, we want him in good shape for tomorrow morning." We could hear noises at the front door. "That's your uncle, I'll get the door."

Uncle R and Raj arrived ten minutes early. Personality profiles have validity. I called upstairs where Ned and Nina were doing who-knows-what. "Ned, time to surface, guests are here."

Everyone congregates in the kitchen getting in my working space. Ned, the goofball, does a sniff sniff motion in the air, "Raj, you wearing perfume?"

Raj looks mortified with Ned outing his cologne. "Oh Raj, don't you look handsome," mother gushes. "I wish men would dress up for dinner more often."

Ned, puffing out his chest, exclaims, "I put on a clean T-shirt."

I have to intervene and usher everyone out of the kitchen. "Okay, ok, Raj you look marvelous." I kissed him on the cheek. "Everybody, please be seated in the dining room. I'm finishing up in here."

"Warning, warning, danger zone," Ned smiles leading the way out of the kitchen.

Raj lingers behind, and asks, "You need any help Amelia?"

He looks so cute. "Well, yes, thank you Raj." I handed him a large spoon. "If you could give this pot a slow stir that would be wonderful. In a moment, or two, we will transfer the bisque into this serving bowl."

The meal was well planned. Nina is a vegetarian so I had a good selection for her. Uncle R the omnivore gets his favourite scalloped potatoes dish. Ned's carnivore cravings come with the pot roast. Two bottles of white, two red wines and all the bases were covered. "Dinner is served."

The cacophony of six voices around the dining room table soothed mum's anxiety. Two glasses of wine helped, too. She was relaxed, waving her arms and pushing food on people, "Nina, have you tried these baked Brussels sprouts?"

"Yes, I have, they are delicious."

"Here, have some more." Mum passed the dish to Ned, the immature juvenile who had to make a gagging face. "Ned, pass the dish to Nina, please."

Nina just smiled and took *one*.

Uncle R, the conversation catalyst, had to say, "Sorry Jedd was not able to join us. He doesn't know what he's missing."

"True, but Raj subs in well, eh?" Ned raised his glass to toast.

Raj quickly replied, raising his glass, "A toast to the chef."

Everyone clinks their glasses. "To the chef!" I give Raj a wink and he begins to blush.

"So what's the deal?" Ned asks. "What's happening tomorrow, and which court is it this time? Is it an all day thing?"

Mother inhales, and I think to myself, "Here we go, Socrates."

"Well, Ned, Shane's first appearance was in the Provincial Court where he was arraigned. The Crown Counsel presented adequate evidence to convince the judge that an indictable offence occurred and Shane has been charged with two counts of murder. Tomorrow we will be in the BC Supreme Court."

"Thought Supreme Court was in Ottawa."

I had to jump in to move things along. "Ned, you weren't listening. BC Supreme Court, Ottawa is federal. BC has three levels of courts: Provincial, Supreme and Appeals."

"Oh, good thing Shane's got you on the team." Ned's humour falls short.

Mother's defence is not needed, but you knew it was coming down the track. "Amelia has been a godsend! Jedd's the first to admit how much help she has been putting this case together!"

"A godsend?"

Mother gives him the dinner table evil eye along with a curt, "Ned, you know better than to start your nonsense."

Oh, this always happens. Mum tells Ned that some things he thinks are funny, others do not. Then Ned enlists all those he knows would think him hilarious. We've done this before, too many times.

Raj, with a bit louder tone than you'd expect, asked, "Seriously, so tomorrow Shane pleads not guilty. What happens next?"

Uncle R is not going to sit quietly, after all he bills out as a *professional talker,* "Well Raj, tomorrow the trial will begin with the Crown Prosecutors reading out the charges and counts against Shane. Their job is to convince the judge and jury *beyond a reasonable doubt* that Shane is guilty. They go first and present evidence, witnesses and ask questions. This is called examination-in-chief. Shane's lawyers then cross-examine each of the witnesses, asking questions to poke holes or show inconsistencies in their evidence. When they have presented all their evidence they will rest their case. After they have closed their case the defence will ask the judge to dismiss the charges because the evidence is insufficient. If the judge thinks there is enough evidence to possibly convict Shane, then the trial proceeds with the defence presenting their side of the story. Their job is to convince the jury that there exists a reasonable doubt that Shane did it."

"That's it?" Raj asks.

"Yes, that's it."

I didn't want to dim the dinner mood, but as second chair I thought at least I should say, "Yes, in a nutshell, that is it. However, we will see how it proceeds."

"You mean the nut does not always crack the way you expect," Ned adds.

"Yes, I guess," I said with a sigh.

Uncle R with the transitional magic touch asks, "Dessert, did I hear there is a fruit cobbler for dessert?"

"Oh you betcha," I replied. "Coffee or tea anyone?"

"Beer for me, if you please, mademoiselle," Ned said with a nodding head.

Mother threw him a stink-eye look, "What, I'm not driving?"

Dessert was served.

Harpreet's Dumbest Day Ever

Shane Bighill is the best friend I have ever known. Met him, Logan, Raj and Ned on my dumbest day ever.

Shane says, "Harry, don't sweat small shit. We all do dumb stuff. Shake it off."

And now here I am sitting in my new fancy wheelchair in a courtroom with my mother holding my hand tightly while we listen to this guy read out murder charges on Shane. He's saying Shane killed two guys in cold blood!

Shane told me not to tell anyone because he is not supposed to tell anyone, but seeing as how I am his friend, he thought I should know. He thinks he might have actually done it. When Ned hears this he gets mad and yells at Shane because "Its not over until its over!"

Doesn't matter, I can't really talk without my communicator machine so Ned does not have to worry about me blabbing anything to anyone. My brain has been disabled, but parts of my mind are working fine. And some days that is a crime unto itself.

I killed Banerjee Malik on the dumbest day of my life. Nobody ever tried to put me on trial to punish me for being stupid and selfish. I wasn't drunk or wasted on drugs when it happened. Shane says that's what happened to him. He drinks too much, smokes way too much weed, and has anger issues.

Shane says his shrink told the court that he is fit to stand for a trial. I'm not fit, can't stand, can't talk without the machine, and they must think there is nothing they could do to punish me anyway. I'm in my own body jail. Shane says he might go to jail. Logan, Ned, and Raj don't want to hear about it. Shane says they are in denial.

If I could re-do or take back that day I'd do it in a heartbeat. Today and every day my heart still beats and bleeds for Banny. It was so stupid. Wasn't planned or anything, it just happened. On that day we were so happy to see each other after being apart. The idea that we would have to part again was agonizing. So for some stupid reason we decided to go all Romeo and Juliet. We tied some fabric pieces together, made nooses, and jumped off stumps facing each other. I watched Banny die. The noose tightened around her neck and she died. The tree limb from which I jumped slowly started to bend and then it snapped, but not before partially asphyxiating me by closing off the oxygen supply to my brain.

Of course, all I remember is watching Banny die. I woke up in a hospital with my mother wailing beside the bed. Evidently, Shane and Logan were the first to find us. They say there was nothing they could do for Banny. She was already dead. Ned had CPR first aid training. He and Raj started working on me while Shane and Logan went for help.

Shane says a helicopter came and took me away. They stood there and watched while Banny was taken away in a black van. At that time they were just little kids with the Boy Scouts. I was nineteen and Banny was eighteen. Time stands still for me now. I'm trapped in this decaying body. In chronological years I'm twenty-nine years old. Physiological years are another matter altogether. Shane says, "Who knows life expectancy for anyone? There are other things to not worry about."

I really hated being in the hospital. It was terrible. I didn't know what was going on, didn't know what was wrong with me, but I did know that Banny was dead. It was entirely my fault.

Shane knew that I knew a lot more than the doctors thought I knew. I could understand some things, just couldn't talk, walk, or feed myself. Shane explained that the boys tried to talk to Banny's family to no avail.

When Shane got a driver's license we would go all over the place in my mother's modified minivan. We went to visit Banny's family. Shane said they needed to forgive to live. They got really angry and Shane got into big trouble for taking me there.

Everyone is all dressed up for court today. Ned's mum got a nice new suit for Shane. The other guys look good, too. Logan's wearing a shirt and tie and he looks grim.

"This is serious stuff, Harry. We're hoping for the best, yet I don't know how it's going to go. The lawyers don't either," Ned explained to me in the hallway before they'd let us in the courtroom.

This stuff really scares me. It would be terrible if Shane went to jail. I likely wouldn't see him anymore. He always came to visit me. He's the best friend I've ever known.

Logan ~
Impaired Seriously

My father is pushing me to get involved at one of his business ventures or at an established company to get some work experience. "Logan you can't sit around all day playing video games," he said with the voice of serious authority. "You have to either go to school or work. One or the other, you are not going to make a living as a gamer." I'm good at games, working sucks, and university gets depressing.

Wendy is pushing too. She wants me to become more *serious* about our relationship. I thought the relationship was proceeding just fine. She thinks differently.

So, my father had a bad reaction when I told him I was seriously impaired. "What?" I'm just having a hard time being serious about stuff and this in and of itself is becoming a problem. Hence, did not make the same mistake with Wendy. Just said, "Let's talk about getting serious later, okay?"

Shane's murder trial is proceeding full speed ahead. And I'm a little stressed out about the whole thing. This is such serious stuff. Although, compared to Shane, my stress level has it made in the shade. I am so anxious. Shane seems as cool as a cucumber. I'm scared shitless. What if they do prove that Shane did it? What if they put him away and throw away the key? Ned says it's not going to happen. What does Ned know, anyway?

This morning the lady crown prosecutor questioned the cops who arrested Shane. After her showing what she said was "incriminating evidence" Amelia cross-examined and pointed out all the "flaws" in their evidence.

Harpreet texts me, "What is going on now?"

Looking over at Harry and his mother sitting in the back row, I shrugged and texted back, "Dunno." Then Wendy reached over to take phone away, she whispered, "No texting in court!"

Raj and Amelia juiced up the computer coprocessor embedded into Harry's wheelchair and now he is texting all the time. Last week Raj and I went to Seattle to buy nanobots, software sticks, and other stuff that didn't make much sense to me. Amelia called a half dozen times to make sure we got it correct. I think Raj and Amelia have got something going on, more than just scientific engineering.

Amelia is the real deal. I've known her all my life. She's Ned's sister and the idea of her and Raj hitting it off is more than interesting. She's three years older than Raj. I'm glad Raj is back in town. I really missed him when he was back in India. Ned, Shane, and I always talked about visiting the Punjab, but it was just talk. It took Shane's murder trial to bring Raj back. His dad is mad and won't speak to him. My dad talks to me too much. Doesn't matter whether he is mad or not it's always nonstop talking about whatever and whenever. Last week he showed up at nine in the morning. I was sleeping, but Raj made him chai and dragged me downstairs so dad could deliver a diatribe.

For a while I sat at the kitchen table pretending to be listening. Whatever he was saying meant nothing, didn't sink in, and went in one ear and out the other. I had to tell him, with as much force and sincerity as I could muster at nine in the morning. "Dad, you need to know, nothing, absolutely nothing, is more important to me right now than Shane's trial. This is a big thing, and I've got a bad feeling about it all." I started crying. Dad and Raj didn't know what to do and I suppose it threw them off balance.

"Hey, hey, hey, Logan," dad put his arm around me. "I'm sorry if it seems like I'm hassling you. It stops today, I've got you. It's going to be okay."

Raj joined in, "Yeah, Ned says things are looking good for Shane."

I sniffled and scoffed, "Ned knows nothing!"

Logan's Pop Got Genetic Jitters

Benji died when Logan was five. Just screwed me up something terrible.
At the time, didn't know how it affected Logan. My therapists, all of
them, over the years, would all say, "five year old kids are resilient."
Of course, Liza's parents, the infamous Shusters, just had to file an
injunction to try and keep Benji alive on life support—indefinitely.

They lost that one, eventually. My lawyers squashed the Shusters.

Liza, real name, Elizabeth, but likely prefers Liza from Judy Gar-
land's daughter, is Logan and Benji's mother, and my ex-wife. She has
never been any help in dealing with these issues. She creates more
issues than can be solved. High-strung people are always difficult to
deal with and who needs the angst? We divorced with difficulty. She
moved to Seattle and I raised Logan the best I could. Logan and Liza
—L and L—don't get along well, either. And it is not for me to mediate between them.

Logan is twenty-two now and going nowhere. He is rudderless,
no set sails in sight, nothing on the horizon. No direction intended
to see. Logan is, however, an accomplished video game player and can
spend countless hours in front of a screen. He holds master gamer
standing. And you know that will take you far these days. Not.

Everyone says Logan looks just like me. Except he is thirty-one
years younger with curly hair and poor posture. Who knows which of

my phobias were passed on genetically and which were environmentally induced? His therapist won't talk to me anymore, despite the fact that I continue to pay Logan's therapy fees. Patient confidentiality, really, I'm his father.

Over the years Logan's been to a half dozen different therapists. Can't make up his mind whether a male or female therapist is best suited for his issues. His mother has not been helpful, either. She adds layers of extra heavy baggage.

Logan has a new girlfriend, Wendy. She has moved in and out of the Larch Street house a couple of times. Logan can be difficult. Nevertheless, I like her. Wendy speaks French, Italian, German and other languages that I don't know. Logan can be difficult. Believe me, I should know, but I definitely wish Wendy well. I think she is good for Logan. Stability is a good thing for a young man. A girlfriend gives him someone to talk with about the things that concern him.

Last week Logan had an old fashioned meltdown at the kitchen table. Although I've seen his meltdowns before, this one was different. I arrived around nine in the morning at the Larch Street house. Even though I am up and working by five, an old stockbroker habit, I never arrive anywhere before nine. His friend Raj has moved home from India to attend Shane's trial. Raj is a great kid. I love talking tech to him. He's staying with Logan and Wendy for a while in Shane's old suite in the basement. A probations court order got Shane to move out of Larch Street and begin living with his sister. Shane does need supervision. Logan has enough problems at the best of times. Now Shane's trial has him overwrought with worries.

Logan and Shane were the ones who found the dead girl when they were camping with the cub scouts. They were only eleven years old at that time. I know that whole thing messed up Logan. Shane already had issues, but he got worse after the Byng thing.

The girl died and the boy lived. Logan and his friends saved the guy's life. It was a Romeo and Juliet scene gone terribly wrong with the girl *dead* in front of them. Afterwards they all became best of friends with the boy they saved. Harpreet Dhaliwal is his name. Ever since that fateful day the boys visit and take him everywhere with them. They modified his wheelchair to make travel easier. Harpreet has massive brain damage yet Logan claims his mind is pretty good. They talk all the time. Raj explained how they have facilitated text messaging and augmented communications.

So you know I'm doing the best I can to keep an eye on Logan, trying to help him find his way in the world, and succeed. It has never been easy and these days seem to get harder.

When he was younger and we lived at the Trimble Street house we bickered too much over too many things. Logan was always making messes and never cleaning up after himself. After he had moved into the Larch Street house things between us improved. He still made messes, but it didn't bother me so much. It wasn't in my face all the time. I sent a housekeeping cleaning crew over once a week.

Nowadays I don't go over to visit everyday, although I'd like to. Trying to give him some space and make like it is his place. After all he is twenty-two. And Wendy and Raj are there. They keep the property acceptably clean and tidy. Shane was not the best at cleanliness. Raj on the other hand is very good. Whether it was mowing the lawn in patterns, vacuuming carpets or mopping the kitchen floor, Raj is the captain of clean housekeeping. We got rid of the visiting weekly cleaning crew when Raj moved into Larch Street.

I've always worried about Logan. Sure, suppose it started to accelerate when Benji died, but likely it is just part of my personality now. So last week when he had a meltdown I took it in stride. We've had these before, nothing new, but this one had a twist. Raj and I did our best to defuse and calm him down. "Sorry Logan," I said, putting my arm around his shoulders in a half hug. "I think you need to rest, get some sleep and call me when you get up. You're tired and these are tough times. We'll get through it, one way or another. We always do, eh?"

Logan looked up at me with a hauntingly blank stare, nodded his head, wiped the tears, "Yeah, you're right, Pop. I need to get some sleep. Call you later."

Raj helped him stumble up from the table and started to take Logan to his room. Raj looked my way holding up his index finger to indicate he wanted a minute with me. I gave a quick thumb up signal and mouthed okay.

While Raj was escorting Logan back upstairs I started cleaning off the table, started the dishwasher and cleaned the refrigerator. I thought about taking out the trash, but didn't want to overdo things. When I took parenting classes for single fathers, the group leader kept saying, "Be a dad, but don't be an enabler."

My dad was a tough guy.

Raj Gill ~
Cone of Silence

The Cone of Silence was Ned's thing. It started when we were little kids and continues still. Ned would tell us something and then say, "Put that under the Cone of Silence." And that meant you could not tell *anyone.*

Everyone universally dislikes rats, and if you rat someone out, then you are the worst of the worst. Rats are bad.

Now to pile on top, Amelia explains the limits of confidentiality and the parametres of privileged communications. "Yeah right," Ned says with more sarcasm than needed, "that's the lawyerly version of the Cone of Silence."

My mother's voice rings in my head, "Raj, mind your own business."

So, I have Logan increasingly freaking out on us and now his father is downstairs, cleaning. I think I have to tell Mr. Meyers some of what I know, but it is hard because the Cone of Silence implications. On the other hand I need help with knowing what the right thing to do is and how to do it.

Ned has always said his sister Amelia is the smartest person he knows. I agree and expect he is probably correct. She is amazing, knows how to get things accomplished, yet not always the most sensitive. Amelia can be rough and tough.

Lately, Logan has been spending more time with Harpreet since Shane's legal troubles have taken up lots of Shane's time. Amelia and I have been working on developing Harpreet's wheelchair computer and augmented speech communication. Before we got involved it was pretty primitive and now we have taught Harpreet how to text message and use the digital augmented communication software.

"Would you like some more tea Mr. Meyers?" I thought it would be good to get him sitting and drinking my style of chai before explaining the Artificial Intelligence Augmented Communication (AIAC) software we've been using with Harpreet. "Or coffee, I can also make some coffee."

"Thanks Raj, your style of chai is the best I've ever had."

"Okay, coming right up now." I started by putting the water on the stove, ground the cardamoms, cloves, and got out clean cups. When everything was perfect, ready to serve, I turned and saw Mr. Meyers deep in thought.

"Here we go," I said softly putting a steaming cup in front of him. "You okay Mr. Meyers?" I asked.

Smiling, he said, "Gerry, call me Gerry, please." He tapped the table with the palm of his hand. "I was just thinking about when Logan was a little kid. He didn't like sleeping much when he was a kid. Seems like he sleeps all the time nowadays."

I nodded my head in agreement.

"Raj, should one of us go up and check on him make sure he actually went to bed? I think he will be better if he gets some sleep, but maybe he's gaming?"

"Yes, good point, I'll go up and check on him." I tiptoed up the stairs and quietly opened Logan's door. He was sound asleep. Whew, too much morning drama already.

Standing at the top of the stairs I took a deep breath and exhaled. Thought about changing my mind and leaving Gerry out of this whole Logan—Harpreet Cone of Silence stuff. Of course Shane sits as an imaginary homunculus over my shoulder and I hear him screaming, "They're trying to ice the field goal kicker!"

English is not my first language and culture is another issue altogether, but I knew what Shane meant because Ned says, "Don't let them psyche you out. NIKE—Just Do It!"

Grabbed a laptop, a pad of foolscap, and headed downstairs to explain why I think the Cone of Silence should be lifted. Even so, the cone is too heavy for me alone. I need support, assistance or at least some assurance that I'm doing the right thing disclosing sensitive data.

When I got back to the kitchen Gerry was cleaning the counters. "More tea?" I asked.

"No, thanks Raj, I'm good. You wanted to talk with me?"

"Yes, I do."

Started by speaking about the stability of personality profiles and significance of behavioural changes. Just some simple little things that start adding up. For example, in the old days Logan was always early for everything, never late. Now he's never on time for anything. Mr. Meyers mentioned Logan hardly slept as a kid, now he sleeps all the time. So certainly seems like some changes, but that's just me.

I opened up the laptop. "Gerry, at this point Amelia Reilly is the only other person I have shown these data points. She's basically okay, yet full of lots of legal mumbo jumbo and privacy rights. Right now she is preoccupied because something is wrong with Shane's star lawyer. He is sick or something. Amelia, her mother and the crown lawyers are all meeting with the judge for in chambers legal stuff proceedings."

He smiled, sat upright. "Oh, trust me, I know about legal mumbo jumbo. Show me what you've got."

Explaining the principles of Artificial Intelligence and Augmented Communications (AIAC) software was easier than I thought it would be. "I'm a math man Raj," Gerry said, tapping his hand on the table. "That's how I did well so in the stock market."

"Yes, mathematically, we use algorithms to predict language patterns and principles."

"Like that damn autocorrect stuff, eh?"

"Well, yes," I explained. "What we are doing with Harpreet's computer coprocessor is gathering language samples, his and those speaking to him."

"Thought the kid couldn't talk."

"He can't," I agreed. "Not in the normal expressive spoken language manner. Harry's larynx and epiglottis were crushed in the accident."

"You're calling his attempted suicide an *accident*?"

I didn't take the bait and just kept explaining how we were using augmented computer communications to enable Harry to speak with a speech synthesizer.

"I get it," he thumped the table, "this is like the Stephen Hawking stuff."

"Yes, in a way that is correct, yet there are distinct differences. At any rate what I wanted to show you are transcripts and audio."

"Okay."

"You see since Shane has been busy with all his legal issues he made Logan promise to spend more time with Harpreet, and he has. Shane knew a lot of what I was doing recording receptive and expressive speech/language samples. I had his consent. Shane did not care. The work was intended to help Harry. I never spoke with Logan directly about my work. He was not interested. Harry knew, but he never communicated to Logan either."

"Raj, you're wearing me out here, where are you going with this stuff?"

"Right," I bobbed my head, "here's the deal, I've got these audio-to-print transcript samples of Logan saying stuff to Harry that is concerning."

"Like what?"

"Like Logan's been thinking he might hurt himself, but differently than Harry."

Gerry gasped, "What?" and grabbed the laptop. "Show me."

So, here we go, I started to show Gerry the parts that were highlighted in yellow. "At this point you hear Logan asking Harry about his suicide attempt and then Logan says he'd do it differently. Harry says don't do it because if he had it do to over he would never have done it in the first place. It was an impulsive mistake. And he failed anyway."

"What does Logan say?"

"Well, this is the concerning part. Logan has a gun and that is how he'd do it."

Gerry started to cry. "I'm sorry Mr. Meyers." I grabbed some tissue to hand him. "I didn't know what to do and didn't think the cone of silence was applicable here."

Gerry touched me on the shoulder and said, "Yes, you've done the right thing Raj, thanks. This is something I needed to know and we'll have to do something but tread lightly. You know Logan."

"Yes, I do."

"Where did he get a gun from? Why oh why?"

"If we scroll down further you can see that's what Harry asks."

"Okay."

"Logan says he bought the gun from some guy he met in Dr. Rossman's waiting room."

"His *therapist*, some guy he met in the therapist's waiting room?"

"Yes, that is what the audio and transcripts show." Gerry was not taking this very well, but I wasn't finished and had to pile on more cone of silence, privacy violations stuff. "Mr. Meyers," I paused and waited for him to sniffle, blow his nose and look at me.

"There's more?"

"Well, yes." I cleared my throat. "Two days ago when Logan was out I found the gun. I carefully started going through his room. The pistol is wrapped in an old t-shirt, bottom dresser drawer. Bullets are in a box in the closet." I paused for a moment. "And there is a sealed envelope under the gun which says: To Be Read After My Death."

Gerry inhaled slowly, exhaled, and dabbed his eyes. "You didn't read the note or take the weapon?"

"No, I didn't."

"Why not?"

"Well, I thought I should, but then I thought it would be attacking the symptom and not the problem."

"What?"

"Well, you know Logan. As soon as he discovered the gun or note was missing he'd go crazy angry and blame Wendy or me for messing with his private stuff and then he'd go get another gun anyway. But, believe me Mr. Meyers; I don't know what I am doing. I don't have a plan or anything. We need to do something, but I don't know what the thing is or who can help us. Do you?"

"No, not yet." He tapped my hand. "We will work it out one way or another. Logan, Logan, Logan, my baby boy is so sad. I knew he was troubled, but I didn't know the extent, and now we are going to have to do something. I'm not losing Logan. He's my son."

Mind over Matter

"Mr. Talbot, you know you are in a state of medical denial, right?" Dr. Quan said, full knowing I was exercising my legal rights and rejecting further treatments. "The mind over matter principle you discussed last month is failing you now. It's not working. Mr. Talbot you are very sick and progressively getting sicker. Your condition worsens everyday. The trajectory of decline is steep and there is no leveling off as you had hoped."

I'm not good at being ill because historically I am seldom sick. And whenever I was ill in the past I would power through it and get the job done. The work was important; pedal to the metal, full speed ahead was all I knew. And now I'm not so sure that strategy was such an ace idea.

All along in my head I figured just as soon as I finished the kid's case I would surrender to their treatments. Tonight it has become evident that I'm not going to make it. I'm fucked. I went to the bathroom to throw up some more blood. Must have blacked out, passed out or something. I don't know, but when I had gained enough consciousness I called Annette Reilly's cell phone and left a message.

"Hello Annette, it's Jedd Talbot calling. Sorry to leave this message and tell you that Amelia is going to have to take the lead in the kid's case. I won't be in court tomorrow. I am ill and will call 911 after leaving this message. They have been holding a bed for me at the UBC hospital. Please forgive me for abandoning you at this stage; it's just that I've run out of runway. Bonne chance."

Health is Wealth

Harvard's Ralph Waldo Emerson said, "Health is the first wealth."

❧

My children are tech wizards. Yesterday Amelia started to goad me about my ineptness with a cell phone. I asked her, "Who taught you how to use a spoon?"

I am connected. I have a home landline, an office direct line, an office secretarial line, and with some pressure I capitulated and took over Ned's old cell phone when he got the fancy new one. Admittedly, I was late joining the cell phone revolution. I didn't need one and didn't want one. Now I wonder how I lived without one.

Hence, at first I smiled when I pulled my cell phone out of my pajama pocket and call display showed *J. Talbot* had called and left a message at 9:47. Last week Amelia had been screwing around with my phone doing *security updates* and the settings were all changed. I do not like or understand military time. 9:47 was showing as 21:47. When I discovered the problem we tried together to reset the phone back to the original settings over the landline. It was no use I couldn't do it. She sent Raj over to do a *housecall* and fix my cell phone. I hate military time settings. 21:48.

Because I seldom give this cell number to anyone I do not receive many calls, and Amelia installed spam call blocking filtres. I mainly use the device for text messages and music. Thus, occasionally when I do receive voicemail I have to remember the stupid sequence Amelia setup so it would be *simpler* to retrieve messages.

Jedd's message threw me for a large loop. I got dressed quickly and drove to the UBC hospital as fast as I could. Of course, at first the medical staff, citing privacy rules, refused to give me any information. Consequently, I pulled out my lawyer credentials and medical markers. "Please call whoever is in charge and tell them to come and meet me at reception or suffer the legal consequences!" I didn't really have any idea of what legal consequences I could bring to bear. I was annoyed at the rejection and was throwing my weight around. I wanted to see Jedd.

Dr. Quan, a middle aged, mild mannered man with greying hair appeared within ten minutes. Holding out his hand to me. "Ms. Reilly, hello, I am Dr. Quan, Mr. Talbot's primary treating physician."

"Yes, thank you." I intended to be firm but conciliatory, as Dr. Quan seemed a nice, reasonable man. "I would like to see Mr. Talbot immediately."

"I am afraid that is impossible at this time."

"Listen Dr. Quan, don't screw with me. I am not in the mood."

"Yes, I understand," he nods, "and your name is on Mr. Talbot's list of visitors. However, he has had a seizure and is currently unresponsive."

"A seizure?"

"Yes, that is correct."

"Well, when can I see him?"

"You may see Mr. Talbot when he has regained consciousness. He is presently in ICU." Dr. Quan held up his palm, "I will get someone to call you."

"Okay."

Telekinetic Times

My mother and I have iterated through various communication modalities through the years. We could not perfect the pager thing, but we tried. "Drug dealers use pagers." She is very good, maybe too good, with email. Recently, through a certain amount of peer pressure and family coaxing, we were able to persuade cell phone use. She would always say, "Why do I need a cell phone? I'm either home or at the office. People can get a hold of me." Ned got a new fancy cell phone and mum took over his perfectly good as new old phone. Now she sends lengthy text messages, too often. Ned nags her saying, "Mum, when you send me a text message you do not need to sign off with Love, Mum. It is redundant. I know you sent it. Your name is on the screen."

Currently, retrieving voicemail is problematic, yet she is superb at leaving messages, often long convoluted messages. My Uncle R asks her to just send him an email instead of voicemail because he is a better reader than auditory decoder. When I was younger often I would let her voicemail messages steep for a while prior to responding. Skinnerian, I know, but if I respond too soon to her message it only encourages more messages.

Tonight, call display shows she called, disconnected, and called again, leaving voicemail. Then thirty seconds later she sent a text message saying: "CALL ME IMMEDIATELY."

Okay, she gets my attention straight off with that type of message. I called without listening to the voicemail. Why bother with voicemail when an all caps text appears. She didn't answer, so I left her voicemail, "Hi mum, it's Amelia calling you back. Okay, call me. I'm here at UBC."

Ten, nine, eight, seven, six, five, four, three, and my phone was vibrating, showing her face on the screen. "Hi mum, whats up?" I asked.

"You have to come and get me!"

"Okay, where are you, and I just need a minute or two to shut things down."

She burst full fledged tears, "No, come now. I need you now."

"Okay, on my way, right now," I said softly trying to be calm. "Mum, where are you?"

"UBC hospital, the cancer parking lot!"

"Just hold on, I'll be there soon, real soon." Although I knew there was not a specific parking lot for the cancer clinic, I had a good idea where to find her. I reached for my jacket, bike helmet, and took off full speed to do whatever was needed to be done. It's my mum, and she is distraught.

The white Volvo wagon was easy to find. She was sitting in the passenger seat head in hands. I slid into the drivers seat, put my arm around her shoulders and asked, "Hey, how you doing? Whats up?"

"Its Jedd," she sighed, "he's got cancer and it's terminal."

"Oh, whoa, oh," I grimaced, "so sorry to hear this. You obviously just found out, eh?"

"Yes."

"Are we able to see Jedd?"

"No, he had a seizure and is in ICU."

"Okay, well," I spoke softly, "let's go home, have a cup of tea, and talk about it."

"Yes, we have court tomorrow."

"No problem," I rubbed her on the shoulder, "tomorrow is still a day away. We'll figure it out."

"Yes, we'll figure it out."

"So just sit tight, I'm going to put the bike in the back hatch and then we'll go home."

"Yes."

I unhooked the quick release lever on my front bike tyre, slid it into the car and climbed back into the driver's seat. "Mum, you need to pass me the car keys."

"Yes, good idea." She opened her purse and passed them to me. "Thank you Amelia. I wasn't expecting this to be so difficult. I have grown quite close to Jedd."

I nodded, "Let's go home, have a cup of tea, and I'll make some calls.

"Okay, good idea," she sniffled back tears, "someone from the hospital is going to call us to say when we can see Jedd."

"Alright, pass me your phone so I can make sure the ringer is activated."

"Good idea."

Quitting or What

❆

"Hi Raj, it's Wendy calling, please call me back when you get this message. Thanks."

Life with Logan has always been challenging, but I love him. He's my guy, yet he is more than moody and I just don't know anymore. The diagnostic label doesn't matter. Whether it is bi-polar mood swings, PTSD, depression, anxiety, mania, attachment disorder or a combination of all the above, Logan has a lot of issues. For a while things with Logan were easier after Shane and I became better friends. Shane says it's stupid to try and understand Logan. He's not understandable.

Sure, yes, I knew about the gun, the note, the pills, for a while before Raj sat me down for an initial heart-to-heart conversation after he *accidently* found the gun, note, and bullets. Raj didn't know about the pills.

"You knew all that and you didn't tell me?" Raj said with such exasperation it was hard to know what to say.

"Sorry, Raj, social work is not easy, linear stuff, eh? What would you have liked me to say?"

He threw his arms up in the air, "Oh, I don't know, maybe you could have said something like: hey, Raj, just thought you might like to know Logan keeps a gun in the house."

"Well, you know now, Logan has a gun."

Raj then went and told Logan's father because "We need all the help we can get here to help Logan."

At first, Mr. Meyers was awfully upset, but all in all he turned out to be helpful. He didn't want to get all confrontational or anything. However, he wanted the gun gone. Like yesterday, gone.

Raj talked him out of going upstairs and seizing the gun. Raj said that would just set Logan off and he'd go get another gun. After that Logan would go ballistic over the idea that we were all conspiring together against him.

Together with Logan's therapist they began working on an intervention plan.

Meanwhile I'm sitting here looking at the second pregnancy test wondering: How did this happen?

Mahjeeroms

Describing the music business Dan Fogelberg sang, "The audience was heavenly but the travelling was hell." ~*Same Old Lang Syne*

※

My daughter, Amelia, gave me the name Mahjeeroms. She got it from her Auntie Harjit who babysat her for a while when she was quite young. (Roughly translated and transformed from the French *bourgeois* to the Punjabi form of *Mahjeeroms* to that of an undisciplined lay-about middleclass miscreant). Of course, Amelia explains it better than me from a linguistic perspective. Oh, the Mahjeeroms I have known.

Way back when we were morphing into a new band. We needed an interesting name and Mahjeeroms seemed to fit well. Everyone in the band quite liked the new name. So, we started billing out as the Mahjeeroms. We took off slowly at first, and then accelerated faster than I thought possible.

The music business and all that goes with it. Whew. We made it, big-time enough.

Nowadays, Ned, Nina, and Parminder are our backup singers for the current iteration of the live Mahjeeroms and upcoming studio album. We are always working on the *next* album, followed by touring to promote the band, the album, and to pay the bills, debts, and commitments.

Last month I convinced Amelia to play some keyboards and sing for three Mahjeerom events because we were *desperate*. Vic Pagliaro had dentistry done and it had gone south. Vic is all fucked up, badly. "Hey, hey, hi, sweetums," I cajoled. "No thing there at all, we can cancel. It's just that Ned said Parm was really counting on the work. She's arranged to broker a truce with her Pops and bro to sit in row two." Certainly, that was true, nobody lies to my Amelia, but Ned has also said that Parm's bro is Amelia's main man these days and she'd do anything to help Raj. She worries he'll go back to India.

Two half rehearsals with me and one with the whole band were required.

When Amelia was young she could get all worked up about "not hearing what she was seeing on the sheet music." And then I'd say, "Don't worry about it, most of us can't hear what we are seeing on sheet music. We just play it. "Ask any studio musician how they feel about music theory."

Amelia could argue convincingly more than anyone I'd ever known, even more so than her mother, the professional argument person with less patience than a piranha. I always give in too easily, can't negotiate worth crap, and just don't care enough to sweat the small shit. Stinky stuff is different, for me, anyway. Sorry, just the way I am. Personality, I guess.

Amelia loves to correct my musical diction and lyrical syntax. It drives her crazy. "You know I am much less than perfect, sweetums?"

Lately, I've been feeling more like slowing the pace down somewhat. And it's hard to do so in many ways, but easier in other respects. How much money do we need? How hard should we work? Travelling sucks. Managing the music and making money have always been the big issues for the Mahjeeroms. In terms of supply and demand economics, the current demand is too high for our supply. I'm tired of travelling town-to-town. Hard work isn't worth it anymore. Professionally, we've arrived, landed, and I'm ready to coast for a while.

I've booked off the next two weeks to go to court and watch Amelia do her legal thing. And they start early in the morning, "Get there before ten or you won't be admitted." Morning people are different and most musicians are not morning people.

Ned says, "Mum's court costume is silk cuz she holds a *Queens Counsel* designation. She's a preeminent lawyer. Amelia wears basic black robes and sits second chair."

I tried to tell Ned that rhythm guitar is just as important as playing lead. You can't have one without the other. Don't get me started on how important a good bass line is to the tune.

"Hey Dad, what do you call someone who hangs around musicians?"

"Don't know."

"A drummer."

"You get that from Amelia?"

"No, Nina."

"Ned, gotta go, my other line is ringing. See you tomorrow."

"Okay, Dad, you want me to call you early?"

"Sure, better safe than sorry."

Although I seldom respond and answer when call display shows a name I do not recognize, the display line read: R. Gill. Who is R. Gill I wondered? I answered anyway.

"Hi Mr. Peters, this is Raj Gill calling."

"Hey Raj what's up?" I asked, I remembered him now. From his breathing, I could tell he was stressed out about something.

"We have some problems and Amelia asked me to call you on this number."

"Hey, no problem, we're cool."

"Amelia wants me to tell you: no court tomorrow."

"Okay, how come?"

"Well, I don't know much, but something is wrong with Mr. Talbot the lead lawyer. He is in the hospital. So, no court tomorrow, okay?"

"Yes, got it Raj," I affirmed. "No court tomorrow."

"Sorry Mr. Peters," Raj sighed, "no time to chit chat, I have more calls to make."

"Okay, we're cool. See ya Raj."

NEWS – Good or Bad

Of course I was more nervous than necessary about meeting with Raj and Logan's father. I am pregnant and Logan is showing signs of suicide ideation. Everything is easy breezy around here, that's for sure. Nevertheless, I am sure my mother will present adequate challenges as well. Dad's been gone too long to wonder anyways.

Three rings and I get voicemail. "Hey Raj, it is Wendy with another message to make sure we are good for meeting Mr. Meyers at lunch today. It's only ten but you know me and time management. Call me back, text or something. Might ride a bike to get downtown, how 'bout you? Call me. K."

Started a food diary because weight gain is likely going to present some issues where I have no plan or understanding. Plus Shane and I had three grilled cheese sandwiches respectively yesterday for a snack. We only stopped because the bread ran out. No booze either, I never drank much anyway. Certainly nothing compared to Shane and Logan. Weed will remain something to think about. Those guys smoke weed all the time.

Using redial I got two rings and a *pickup*, no voicemail, a *pickup*. "Hello Wendy, how you doing?" Thinking to myself: Everyone has call display.

"Fine, Mr. Meyers, just fine," I answered with a grimace he could not see. I thought I'd get voicemail, but he picked up.

"Call me Gerry, please."

"Thanks, Gerry, just checking in about lunch. You hear from Raj?"

"No, haven't heard from him today, but he's working hard up at UBC."

"Oh yes," I moaned. "Working hard, real hard, yeah that's for sure."

"Noon, see you at noon."

"Yes, noon it is. See you at noon."

Pacing around the place all I could think was whether it is good news or not Logan is going to be a father and I'm telling his father before I tell him. You know that is a fucked up situation for sure. Who knows Logan's reaction?

When I told Shane he screamed with delight, "Logan's gonna be a Dad. That means I'm an uncle!"

Yeah, three steps removed, an uncle.

Oh good, time flies, its 10:30 now. Almost noon.

Time to Step Up

Chief Judge Beverly McLachlin said, "Judges do not like surprises, unless, of course, it is a pleasant surprise. Otherwise, not wise to drop a surprise on the judge."

⁂

"Mum, just close your eyes for a couple of hours. We're going to need you to be rested and in good shape for tomorrow morning. We are going ask Judge Wallace for an extra bit of time to put things together. We need a recess to assess where Jedd was and where we are going next. He was the lead lawyer, a star who has already taken us far, but he's done now. Taking over from Jedd will be difficult; even so, we can do it. You are going to be the lead lawyer, but I can help. We'll be just fine. Don't worry. We can clear the bar."

Finally, after getting mum tucked into her bed for the *third* time I got started making calls. First call was to Raj. When delegating, or walking to the barn, one always goes for the most reliable, trusted horse at hand. At least that is what my gramps would say—farm talk. Raj could be persuasive or assertive or aggressive, whatever was needed to get things done. He's good that way.

Second call's to Nina. It is her responsibility to explain what is going on to Shane. In my estimation the guy is some sort of a savant and I never know how he'll react to news that some might see as negative. Better Nina deal with him sooner rather than later. No court tomorrow means he can sleep in and that will be attractive.

Word-wise, I knew the third call to my uncle would be time consuming, but he always gives good advice and is about the only person I know who will tolerate my style of the legal Socratic method of problem solving. Last year, together, we downloaded him an Internet law degree from the North Pacific Professional School of Law. Thus, we now call him a legal expert with institutional documentation. His wife knows more; still, we leave her as the ace in reserve. She holds the final vote. Compared to her we know nothing.

"Sorry Uncle R," I quickly explained. "I can hear Ned and his friends have arrived downstairs. I have to go get the noise down. Don't want those guys waking mum. I need her to sleep for a couple hours. We've got work to do here."

"Yeah, yes," he snorted. "You got this going. You are in the groove and now just bring it to the finish line. See ya tomorrow. I'll bring coffee. Oh, and I'm bringing Harjit, too."

"Conflict," I exclaimed. "Auntie Harjit can't come to court!"

"No, doh, oh, so," double snort, "She's coming to the family function for post courtroom family debriefing. Family, that's not a conflict."

Changing Chairs

Ilka Chase said, "The only people who fail are those who do not try."

⚘

Using Seattle Seahawk football analogies, I explained to Shane how losing the lead lawyer was going to play out. "Plenty of time on the clock!"

"Ned, you know nothing, but my sister says your sister is the smartest person she has ever known."

"Good, cuz Amelia's captaining up for us."

"How so?"

"Okay, so you know how the Seahawks say *next man up* when someone goes down and gets hurt on the field?"

"Yeah."

"That's what we're doing now. Except we want my mum to think she's in charge. Turns out the Internet law degrees downloaded by my sister and Uncle R are not worth the recycled paper they printed them out on. They are only legal theorists, not real lawyers. Not called to the bar is their problem."

"That sucks."

"Naw, that's nothing," I patted Shane's shoulder. "My mum wears silk legal gowns. She's a preeminent lawyer. We're good here, cruising on an ebbing tide."

Strategizing Stages

Janis Joplin, the great blues singer from Texas declared, "Do not compromise yourself. You are all you have got."

꘎

I was sound asleep, a deep sleep level four or five when Logan bursts into the bedroom blurting, "Shane's lawyer is down! Wendy, get up, my dad's on his way over here. He's gonna pick us up and we are on our way over to Ned's house. We gotta do some serious strategizing."

Shaking the cobwebs towards a level of consciousness, I mumble, "Okay, I'm coming, but I'm pregnant, and I do nothing *quickly* until the kid comes."

"Yeah, good, yeah," he wheezed between tears. "Ned says next man up."

"Logan!" I scolded, "No crying, that's not going to help. I'm out of bed now, but not going anywhere until I shower. Tell Gerry to put the kettle on when he gets here."

"I can do that," he said with a positive tone. "I can do the kettle."

"Logan, what's the Nike slogan."

"Yeah, yes, I'm doing it."

In the shower, thinking to myself, you know those sniffer dogs that can detect cancer, bedbugs, and airport contraband? Shane is just like that. He told me a couple of weeks ago that he knew something was wrong with the Jeddster, but people only got angry if he spoke about it. Go along to get along that's our motto.

Our best friend is like a frigging sniffer dog, go figure. Nevertheless, no complaint from me, Logan has been a prince. We held an intervention, I told him I was pregnant and whether he liked it or not we've got a kid coming in eight months or so. You are going to be a father.

Gerry went crazy with glee. "I'm going to be a grandfather!"

He and Logan are bugging the crap out of me to call the kid "Benji Meyers."

"And if the kid is a girl? I ask.

"*Banny*," Logan pleads, "If the kid is a girl we could call her Banny!"

"Logan, you know that list of things we need to talk about."

"Yeah."

"Page three, picking the kid's name is on page three."

"Okay."

"Kettle on?"

"Yes, kettle on."

My Sister is a Hacker

B.F. Skinner, the most famous of operant conditioning psychologists said, "The way positive reinforcement is carried out is more important than the amount."

⸭

My sister Parm and her crazy little friends are the absolute worst hackers I have ever known. Amelia, however, sees them as useful and consequently we have hired them to work in the UBC Omnibus Lab as well as Data Input/ Info Processing Analysts for Shane's case.

Amelia suggested I should give them a good-sized cubicle at the northeast corner of the lab. Nina says we are under utilizing that area. Because Parm and her friends are nineteen I think that is what makes them the way they are in terms of coding and computer programming. Parm says she is only copying me. "And what did mum say about *lying*?" I ask.

"She says Professor Raj is a doofus who does not pay enough."

"Never said I was a professor and you little missy receive more than enough pay!"

Before Amelia re-deployed me to coordinating contacts due to Jedd Talbot's sudden illness we were working our way through surveillance camera images with concentric circle algorithms from where Shane was arrested and where the two dead bodies were found. Some cameras are susceptible to public domain viewing and others require subterfuge. The girls specialize in subterfuge.

Science is not necessarily cumulatively linear. Big *S* science people understand this well whereas applied science people often want results to flow more smoothly. Parminder and the girls are a good mixture and get the general gist of what we are doing with data analyses. They seem to almost feed off one another. They are self-starters with good results so far.

Just need someone to yell BINGO, soon.

Many Hands Make Light

The great psychotherapist Albert Ellis said, "Freud had a gene for inefficiency, and I think I have a gene for efficiency."

When Amelia explained how she planned a dual degree *programme of* study in law and medicine at UBC, many people were skeptical, but I knew better. Call it a mother's intuition or experience; I knew enough to stay out of her path. The admissions and admin people took it between the eyes. Amelia is headstrong, definitely determined and when she decides she is going to do something just get out of the way.

"Time isn't real you know," a nine year old Amelia shouted at me with too much intensity to tolerate. Back then I thought she was too young to unload logical nuances to get me to comply with her demand-of-the-day. "You people just make up these constructs to control us!"

"Us?" I asked with true innocence.

"Ned and me, but mostly me. Ned drank the Kool Aid already! You mind control him."

"I can't control you Amelia. I'm doing the best I can, trying to guide you along the way. It is a parent's prerogative."

Nowadays, as a grownup, when she says, "I will be there in a minute or two," she arrives quite quickly. Time management skills are nothing to her now. She's good with time—whatever that concept is to those of us stuck on time.

Don't really know how long I was sitting stifling tears, head in hands at the hospital's parking lot when Amelia tapped on the car's window and slid into the driver's seat. "Hey, how you doing? What's up?"

I was purposely sitting in the passenger's seat. Old school lawyering suggests that sitting behind the steering wheel could connote care and control of the car. Cops are always pushing that concept. No one buys it, but I sit in the passenger's seat under the auspices of safe, not sorry.

"It's Jedd," I sighed, "he's got cancer and it's terminal."

"Oh, whoa, no," Amelia grimaced, "so sorry to hear this. You obviously just found out, eh?"

"Yes."

"Are we able to go inside and see Jedd?"

"No, he had a seizure and is in ICU."

"Okay, well," she spoke softly, "let's go home, have a cup of tea, and talk about it."

"Yes, we have court tomorrow." I reminded her.

"No problem," Amelia rubbed me on the shoulder, "tomorrow is still a day away. We'll figure it out."

"Yes, we'll figure it out."

"So, just sit tight for a sec, I'm going to put the bike in the back hatch and then we'll go home."

Her stupid bike is worth more money than my car—I drive an old Volvo. Amelia rides her bicycle everywhere; rain, shine, or darkness, she rides.

Thank goodness because it was so reassuring to see her. Amelia is my safety ace. She knows what to do and how to do it. "Just take me home, okay." I sniffled.

Amelia nodded, shifted gears, and said, "We are on our way, Jose."

Three Sided Stories

"Life is what happens while you are busy making other plans." ~John Lennon, *Beautiful Boy*

꙰

When I was a little girl, spending time with my Auntie Harjit was the best thing in the world. Actually still is, but the world spins on and we are older now, with too many time crunches, and commitments, along with regular life's to-ing and fro-ing, you know, everyday activities take up a lot of time. Childhood ends too soon.

As a little kid my mum would periodically have an out-of-town endeavour, and every now and then she took a couple solo vacations, Ned would sojourn with Uncle R and I would do girly-girl stuff with Auntie Harjit. Age twelve I got my first pedicure, nails polished, and a tonne of tea. It was terrific. We would alternate speaking in French and Italian. It was the beginning of my legal education. Learning is easy when you are young. Bias always becomes an age correlation.

Thinking back, I was quite young when Auntie Harj explained that there are three sides to a story in court: The defence tells their side, the prosecution presents their perspective, and then there is the *truth.* The judge's job is to listen and figure out where the truth sits. And that was what her job was all about. It was a good job, certainly better than scrubbing toilets, which was the only job she could get as a teenager. "Don't be a fool, stay in school." That's what the other cleaning women told her.

So, Jedd is off the case now and it has fallen on me to tell Shane's side of the story in court, from our perspective. What could go wrong, eh?

"Mum, time to wake up now," I said, while lightly jostling her shoulder and brushing her hair off her face. "We have court this morning." She went out like a light last night once I finally got her into bed for the third time. Of course, I did not know she had taken a Temazepam sleeping pill. Also, at that point I had no idea she was so close to Jedd. Even worse, I had no idea she had *sex* with Jedd. Too much info from mum was one thing, legal ethics notwithstanding. Then she says *she loves him.* Okay, this is already complicated, but adding another layer won't matter now, I guess.

"What time is it?" she groaned.

"It's seven."

"Okay, any word about Jedd?"

"No, too soon."

"What does that mean?"

"Still in ICU, still in a coma. Dr. Quan says too soon for an updated prognosis. Mum, Jedd is very ill and things are really not looking good."

She started crying softly. "Whoa, oh, oh," I tried to offer some sort of comfort, but to no avail. "You can stay home today. It's okay, I can handle court this morning."

"No, no, I'm coming." She sniffled and said, "We've got work to do."

I smiled, "Pitter patter better get at her." Our old mantra seemed to help. She started to get out of bed and headed for the shower.

"Don't dawdle, okay," I reminded her because sometimes she takes way, way too long to get ready with a shower, makeup procedures and a power suit wardrobe ensemble to be assembled in stages. She's always been that way.

My generation does it differently.

Real Time No Rehearsals

Saskatchewan's Joni Mitchel sang, "Don't it always seem to go, that you don't know what you've got till it's gone." *Big Yellow Taxi*

᛬

Using the speakerphone I explained, "Uncle R picks up mum, and Amelia leaves early with me." I exhaled slowly. "Getting Amelia to court is my responsibility and Shane is yours. You can't be late, right?"

Nina snickered at me, "Ned, we won't be late, but thought all we were asking for was a recess?"

"We are," I explained. "There is a possibility that it will not be granted and then it becomes an appeal court issue. But, *we* feel confident."

"Confidence is good, right?"

"Oh yeah, we are not intimidated by the Crown's high flyers." I assured her, but we knew these things are complicated.

And at that point Amelia click clacks down the stairs, "Who you talking to?"

"Nina."

"Oh great, pass the phone," she held out her hand. "Hey Nina, how you doing?"

"We're good, getting ready to go and we won't be late, don't worry about us."

"Thanks," Amelia pivoted over to the fridge for orange juice. "Expect we will get some time to prepare our side now that Jedd's gone."

"Jedd died?"

"No," Amelia grimaced. "Not yet, but he's quite sick and my mother is a mess, feeling bad about the whole thing."

"Bummer."

"How's Shane?"

"He's fine, you want to speak to him?"

"No, we're leaving now. Does he need to speak to me?"

Nah, he's fine. Putting on some perfume Raj gave him. Raj claims it is his *lucky* cologne."

"Oh, yeah, Raj is a lucky guy, for sure. See you later."

"Later gator."

"In a while crocodile."

Amelia started grabbing keys, papers, books, an apple and who knows what else to throw into her large backpack. Looking over at me, "You ready?"

"Yes."

"And you are wearing the blue blazer I got you, right?"

"Yes, just getting it now." I quickly ran to my room, looked to see where it was and put it on. "Let's go," I snorted, but she was already out the door stuffing the gear into the back hatch of her mighty Mini Cooper.

"I can drive?" I asked, trying to be helpful.

Amelia smiled, "Naw, thanks, we're in a bit of a hurry today. I'll drive, directions get tricky downtown."

Uncle R taught us both how to drive a car because mum could not without having a panic attack. She still slams on the brakes while sitting in the passenger's seat where no brake pedals exist.

On my eighteenth birthday Uncle R gave me a motorcycle and a gift certificate for BC Safe Motorcycle Riding Training course in Ladner. I went crazy with gratitude, happiness and extreme glee. Mum went the other way, thinking he should have asked her permission first.

When confronted he just replied, "Why, you would just say no anyways. No sense asking. Besides, Ned is eighteen!"

Amelia got her first red mighty Mini Cooper on her eighteenth birthday under the auspices that she would help mum by driving me to school *sometimes* and picking me up late nights when needed. Simple enough for Amelia her to comply, but not always. Usually mum and Amelia haggle over everything. It's always been that way ever since I can remember. And I have a normal memory unlike splinter skill Amelia's memory that is well superior to any elephant on the planet! She forgets nothing.

Amelia drives pretty fast so I start the small talk to ease my apprehension. "Mahjeeroms this weekend," I reminded her.

"Yeah, you guys backup singing?"

"Have to," I smirked, "Parm needs the dough."

"You doing any solos?"

"Maybe," I shrugged. "I get a little stage fright and self-conscious with the solos."

"What, your solos are the best." Amelia wags her finger at me.

"You're just saying that."

"Everyone says the same." She smiles over at me, "Nina says your singing is spectacular!"

"Nina, right."

"Dad too."

"Dad doesn't count."

"Why not?"

"He's Mr. Mahjeerom and whatever I do gets a gold sticker."

"He's always critical of me!"

"You bring it on yourself."

"Do not."

"Did I tell you grandpa is going to be in court this morning?"

"No, what?"

"Yeah, he chartered a plane and got in this morning."

"Nothing is happening in court today. We're asking and expect a couple of days recess to prepare now that Jedd is off the case."

"He doesn't care. Maybe he's doing it for Mum."

"Gramps is a retired Manitoba professor," she snorted. "Professors get paid dick."

"Yeah, he's old," I explained. "Can't take it with you and be the richest coffin in the cemetery. Mum and Uncle R are cash copacetic. So, just be cool, okay. This is a big deal for him."

"Gramps in court," she whispers. "Now I am nervous."

The Time That is Taken

"Go out on a limb, that's where the fruit sits." ~Amelia Jean Reilly

⁂

My older brother Randal showed up on time, but he was driving his stupid two-seater Austin Healey Sprite. I hate that car. It is a death trap. However, I was happy he was driving me this morning.

Although Amelia asserts I am a control freak, I just don't think so. Randal says, "Amelia is a first born, they're the worst."

"Oh, you should know!"

Truth is Randal has always been helpful with Amelia. He reminds me, "Remember when you were pregnant and Amelia was kicking *all the time?* You had no control then, what makes you think you have control now?" And those words of wisdom were delivered when Amelia was five years old.

Jedd's firm has a big office in Vancouver and another in Montreal. Lots of preferred parking at the Vancouver office, which is only one block from the courthouse. My usual parking spot is five blocks down the road. And, of course, wouldn't you know it, pouring rain today.

We arrived at the preferred parking area and I saw Amelia's Mini Cooper parked in Jedd's spot. Nina's electric Smart Car parked beside the Mini. I felt a sense of relief knowing they were here and *on time.* Took Randal up to the forty-fifth floor and introduced him to Nicole, the receptionist.

"Nice to meet you Dr. Reilly," Nicole smiled. "Angela has been expecting you. She is coming down the hall right now."

Blink your eye and Angie is there standing behind you. "Good morning Ms. Reilly, Mr. Talbot sent me a message yesterday instructing that you have full access to his office and files. Please, follow me." Angie pointed down the hall. "I have the files laid out for you."

Isn't that just like Jedd, I thought to myself. In ICU but sends out paralegal instructions somehow. How does he do that? "Thanks Angela." She tilts her head, forces a smile, "Just let me know if there is anything you need." She knew Jedd was ill, yet not to this extent.

I turned to the big oak desk, "We've got twenty minutes until court starts. I'll pull some papers together in case we need them."

Randal flopped on the couch. "Sure, it only takes a couple of minutes to get to Smythe Street from here." He drummed his fingers nervously. "Dad's here."

"What?"

"He chartered a plane, arrived a few hours ago." Randal sighed. "He says no way was he going to miss this."

"You should have told him nothing is happening today."

"I told him, and Harjit told him, too. Doesn't matter, he's here. No pressure, eh?"

Looking at my brother sprawled on the oversized leather couch Jedd and I made love on was a little emotional and some tears trickled at the thought, "Okay, let's go." I put on my coat. "Can't believe dad's showing up."

"He's doing it for Amelia."

"Really?"

"Really."

Randal got up with a grin, "Everyone loves Amelia."

Happy to See You, Too

"Yoko did not break up the Beatles, it was John." ~Dr. W.A. Reilly, Sr.

❧

I don't visit Vancouver very often, although I know I should. It is always nice to see the family, but it's always raining. Today was no exception. Don't think I've ever been here without rain. Of course, Annette points out the spuriousness of my assertion.

Even though I had plenty of time to spare I was suddenly in a rush to get to the Smythe Street Court House. Then, once I got there, I had to find the right room and scramble for a good seat before the proceedings started. I spotted a good seat on the correct side of the courtroom and plunked myself down. Took a couple of seconds to realize I was sitting beside Thomas Peters, Annette's ex-husband.

"Good morning Dr. Reilly," Thomas stuck out his hand. "Nice to see you."

I agreed, shaking hands, "Nice to see you, too, Thomas. You are looking well."

"Thanks."

"I've got all five Mahjeeroms albums. Really like the last one. Saw my grandson Ned's name on the credits."

"Ned's a magnificent singer."

Just then Annette turned around, looked at us, gave both of us the stink-eye look, put her index finger to her lips to indicate: Be silent.

"Guess things are getting underway now."

"Dunno, hope so."

The bailiff called the court to order, Judge Wallace walked in, sat down, and we followed suit.

She looked pretty solemn, slowly started speaking. "I have met with the Defence and Crown in Chambers this morning. Unfortunately, Mr. Talbot has been taken ill and the defence has filed for additional time to prepare due to Mr. Talbot's illness. Despite the fact that this trial has already had more delays than I would prefer, I have considered the request and decided we will adjourn until next week at this time." She got up and walked out.

Thomas turned to me, "This is good, right?"

"Yes, I guess," shook my head and shrugged, "I'm an anthropologist, legal stuff baffles me."

"Ned is singing this Saturday at the Granville Club."

Slapped Thomas on the shoulder and said, "I'll be there, wouldn't miss it for anything." We all started shuffling out of the crowded courtroom.

"You doing dinner tonight?"

"Yes, of course, you?"

"Well, we're still negotiating the details."

"Whatever," I held out my hand. "Great to see you."

"Thanks."

Fourteen for Dinner

"Knowing something is one thing, understanding is another." ~Dr. H. Lee Swanson, Distinguished Professor, University of California.

❧

"You've invited fourteen *people over to our house for dinner tonight!"*

"Actually it's sixteen if you count Parm and Mrs. Gill, but because they are doing all the cooking, catering, setup and organizing, maybe they don't count and it is *only* fourteen."

"Who is coming?"

"Who I invited and who arrives are different things."

She looked at me with exasperation, moaned, "Amelia."

"Okay, well, there's you, me, Ned, Nina's bringing Shane."

"That is good I need to speak to Shane. Who else?"

"Who else do you need to speak to or who's invited?"

Got the stinkeye look, "Logan, his dad, and Wendy."

"Logan's father is coming?"

"Yeah, they are the tightest of tight these days. They go every-where together."

"That is so nice, after all they have been through," she shook her head. "That's eight, who else?"

"Angela, Uncle R, Auntie Harjit."

"Angela and Harjit are coming?"

"Confirmed."

"Oh, that is wonderful, happy to hear that. Okay, we're at eleven, who else?"

"Raj, Gramps, and dad."

"You invited your *father?*"

"No, Ned did."

"Okay, fine, wonder if he'll come."

"Yes, he confirmed with Ned. They are rehearsing two new tunes for us before or after dinner or during dinner. I don't know which, but I just said whatever. I might play standup bass."

"Wow, alright, but how's this going to work? Our dining room ta-ble can't seat all those people. There's not enough room for everyone."

"It's not a *sitdown* dinner. We're doing it buffet style. The dining room table gets pushed into the corner, chairs laid about the place, and we have food stations. People serve themselves, and sit or stand wherever they want. It'll be great, trust me!"

"Do I have a choice?"

"Oh shit, just thought of something, I forgot Harpreet. I have to go invite him. You and I can talk further later."

Thinking to myself, how did I forget Harry? I messaged in with Nina and she reports back immediately, "Relax, Logan goes every-where with Harry, Wendy, and his dad. They will all be there. And Raj says they are *always* early!"

Mum retreated to her home office to do whatever it was she thought needed doing. I got started on the tasks I needed to complete before Parm and the catering crew arrived. Before I knew it I could hear the beep beeping horn from the Gill's Mini Van. They pulled into the driveway.

Mrs. Gill was at the wheel, Raj riding shotgun (no navigating needed), Parm and her crew were in the back seat. The Middle English term chockablock full certainly applied to their load. I couldn't believe how much food they had brought. Mrs. Gill, the majordomo, starts sending our instructions even before the front door to the house has opened. "Do not start unloading until I have a look-see at how we will setup. Everything has a proper place to station."

Mrs. Gill was marvelous! She put everything together, directed the setup, and the food was fantastic. The aromatic flavours wafted throughout the house. Even my mother was impressed with the efficiency and excellence of the food's display, and taste sensations. No need to sit down and eat when you could circulate through the food stations. "Its better this way." Parm's friends were all dressed up, cruising the room with serving trays.

The evening progressed well without any hiccups. At one point I saw my mum forehead to forehead with Shane. They were discussing serious stuff, but they were happy. Mum found out that Jedd was successful in getting Shane's confession thrown out and excluded from the jury. The cops had coerced the confession. They had pulled Shane out of bed at two in the morning and he'd say anything to go back to sleep. Good work Jedd, we'll take it from here.

Earlier I had asked Ned if he was going to sing before, during or after dinner. The best I could get from him is, "Dunno, it's dad's call."

"How so?"

"He has to feel the right vibe to play these days. He's a slight celebrity and he feels the performance pressure."

Whatever, Ned says stuff like that all the time. However, I was happy when dad finally came through the door. He looked good.

"Nice chapeau dad," I complimented, and asked, "Can I hang up your jacket?" Although I knew, dad never takes his jacket off. Mum came barging through, knocking me out of the way. "Good evening Thomas," she gestured wildly, "May I take your jacket?" He just shook his head, smiled, and followed me to the kitchen.

During dinner, while Raj was standing next to me explaining the difference between roti, flatbreads, and chapattis, Ned came prancing by dragging my prized standup bass. "You gonna help me out on bass, or do I let Logan?"

Ned knew I'd never let that galoot Logan Meyers anywhere near my bass. Actually, we had earlier agreed to *only* doing five tunes. Didn't want to exploit a captive audience. One Dylan tune for Auntie Harjit, a Gordon Lightfoot ballad for mum, Ned's two new tunes, and Logan's going sing a song for Wendy. That's the plan. Encores are always open for discussion.

Dad and Ned had agreed on an acoustic set, although Ned would still prefer to go electric if he could. It's a small space and acoustic is appropriate. Ned tuned up the red sunburst Gibson Hummingbird guitar and dad pulled out the Larrivée Parlour guitar. My bass is an old Italian spruce carved from a single tree. Not like modern laminated ones that sound so shallow. It was a gift from my father so many years ago. Nothing else sounds as fully deep bass as this one made by the Maggini family.

Making music with Ned and dad is something I've done all my life. Second nature stuff, music with these two; I know what they are going to do before they do it, but they get perturbed if I bring it up. Improvising is important to them. Dad wrote *Bingo Bango* when we were little kids. It's always been one of Ned's favourite tunes of all time. He sings lead and belts it out, but nicely, not forced or contrived.

Ned has good music instincts. Music is his native language. He *feels* the notes and rhythms, cadence and tempo come naturally, and he doesn't worry or care the way I do over musical issues. He can read sheet music, but prefers improvising. Technical theory or music structure bores Ned. "Lets just play, and could you turn it up a notch?" Sometimes they ruin the poem with too much analysis.

We played a few tunes, taking turns with solos, but dad is always reluctant to solo show off. As a slight celebrity he doesn't feel the need to do too much. He was only playing with us tonight because Ned asked him to—too many times to refuse.

After a rousing encore version of *Bingo Bango* Ned took a bow and said, "Thanks, hey everyone, let me call on a real musician Logan c'mon up here and sing us a song? Logan wrote *Oxford Comma*."

Everybody turned and looked at Logan. He just waved his hands and said, "Naw, you sing the comma song Ned. You're on a roll."

"What?" Ned said mockingly, "It's your song Logan, no one does it the way you do. And, don't we have a little announcement that we'd like to get out before blabbermouth Shane Bighill, who cannot keep a secret, starts telling everyone!"

Logan's dad patted him on the shoulder and gave him a nudge; Raj shouted out, "C'mon Logan, let's hear you sing the comma song."

Logan sauntered up to the front, waving his arms, he smiled and said, "In his novel *Tender is the Night,* F. Scott Fitzgerald that he thought love is all there is or should be. And, of course, I agree. This is the *Oxford Comma* and it's for Wendy."

Logan sang his guts out. He was fantastic. He brought the whole room to tears. And then at the end he said, "Wendy, would you care to say anything to our friends this evening."

Wendy was on the spot. Shane yelled, "C'mon Wendy, whats the word?"

She walked up and took Logan's hand, "Oh well, we were going to wait a while longer but now's as good a time as any to let you know," Wendy paused, "Logan and I are going to have a baby!"

Shane screamed, "Yeah, Logan's gonna be a father!"

"Yeah, yeah, Shane's going to be an uncle!" Logan replied.

"A crazy uncle," Raj added.

Logan bobbed his head back and forth smiling, blew us a kiss, and said, "Thanks, we're working on baby names." Wendy gave a scowl and Logan caught her elbow in his ribs.

Everyone milled about with congratulatory hugs, kisses, and backslaps. The evening wore on with more drinks, food and good times. Who knows what time people trickled out because I went to sleep at two. Just too tuckered out to go any further.

We had fourteen for dinner and my mum would be the first to tell you, "That worked out well, eh?"

"Good night Mum."

Shane ~ Blodfresych

"The Welsh word for cauliflower is Blodfresych."

※

We were only eleven and Amelia was fourteen when she explained that the guy we found in the woods was the same as a vegetable. And even though my sister Nina says Amelia is the smartest person she knows, the truth is that Amelia does not get it right every time. She does not hit a homerun every time at bat, but her average is admirable.

She sure was wrong about Harry. Yes, of course, he got pretty fucked over from the accident, however he was no vegetable! Harry, next to Ned, is the smartest guy I know. I don't know where to put Logan and Raj. They have smarts all over the place, but mismatched compared to Ned. He explains stuff to me differently than Logan who is always condescending. Ned's the one who explains, "Harry had an accident and to speak of it differently is just mean. Nobody likes mean people!"

Amelia is my main lawyer now that Mr. Talbot got sick. Her mum has an important role, yet everyone can see that Amelia runs the show. Nina says this a good thing and "We're going to be okay. Just hang in there, because this is not a *one act play.*" I just say okay. Nina always has my best interests at the front of her mind.

Last night at the dinner party, Logan and Wendy announced that she is pregnant. I thought everyone already knew, evidently not true. The announcement was a big deal. Later that night Logan and Wendy asked me to be the kid's Godfather. I said a quick no cuz I'd be a better uncle. Ned needs to be the Godfather. He'll be real good at that.

Wish my dad were still here. He knew what to do, and when to do it. "Timing is everything."

Logan spazzed out on me the other day when all I was trying to do was talk to him about the idea of *bad timing.* Like my parents had bad timing. If dad had gone to the cheeseburger place for a double they wouldn't have had an accident.

Dad and I had a cheeseburger-eating contest when I was fifteen. He did three; I did four and said that's it, no more. I could've done five, but barfing would've disqualified the win.

If we'd reached Harry earlier he wouldn't have had his accident. And at that point Logan snapped, cursed me out severely, and then he took off slamming the door behind him. A few hours later he comes back crying, saying he's sorry. His dad did the same stuff in the old days. You know, get mad, stomp off, and the discussion was over, finished, and fucked up.

"Shane, you want to talk about Harry?"

"No, it's okay," I explained. "Just theorizing, nothing more than that. Ned's going to be a professional theorist."

"Yes, he is going to get paid modest money to theorize."

"Good work if you can get it, eh?"

"I love you Shane." And then he starts crying again.

"Hey, hey, yoh, so, buddy," I pulled him in for a bear hug. "We're going to be okay Logan. This isn't a one-act play. You gotta hang in here. I'm gonna be an uncle. You'll be a dad."

Thinking to myself, "Hope Amelia hits a homer for me."

Sr. Psych and all that goes with it

Albert Schweitzer said, "Ethics is nothing else than reverence for life."

❧

Way back when I was a young psychologist I worked hard took referrals from everyone for just about everything. Working hard seemed the right thing to do. After all, it had been difficult securing a psychologist's license, PhD, internship, and the exams to hang out the shingle. Sometimes I was over my head and invoked the when-in-doubt-refer-it-out principle. I knew who could do what in our community, sharing the load made things lighter.

As a senior psychologist nowadays I do not work very hard, seldom take new files, and close as many old files as ethically copacetic. With all the comings and goings in the past few weeks I had completely forgotten about suggesting Paula Farrow have her brother call me about his PTSD symptoms. That is, until retrieving voice mail and email: Brent Farrow had covered the bases.

"Hello Dr. Reilly, this is Brent Farrow leaving you *another* telephone message. My sister Paula suggested email might work better with you so I will do that too. Paula said you were the one who told her that if you do nothing then *no thing* would happen. She says you can help me understand some of my difficulties. I saw that guy with red hair kill those two guys who were calling out racist names. Last week when I went to watch the court case I saw you sitting with the wheelchair guy. You don't really look much like the picture Google posts. Please give me a call. Thanks."

Ethically speaking, I couldn't find a way to refer Brent to someone else. There are so many fine psychologists who treat PTSD these days. However, Brent says he saw me in court. And he is Paula's brother. I will call him tomorrow, for sure, first thing in the morning.

Raj ~

Toothpaste Put Back in the Tube

At age twenty-four, Coos Bay's Steven "Pre" Prefontaine died shortly after midnight when his orange MGB flipped while driving home along Skyline Boulevard just a little east of the University of Oregon campus. Pre was one of the greatest middle and long-distance runners ever to toe the line. Steve said, "I do it because I can, I can because I want to, I want to because you said I couldn't."

❧

Sleep hygiene means nothing to my sister Parminder. She and her crazy friends sit around, laptops open, cell phones in hand, *all night long,* drinking tea and nibbling on tapas type things. Their favourite haunt is the twenty-four hour Rufus Café at Dunbar and Alma Street.

My biorhythms are different, I get up early at seven-thirty in the morning and the day gets started. Hence, I'm usually in bed before midnight. I need an adequate amount of sleep in order to function. Before going to bed I turn all my devices off and my cell phone is put on do not disturb mode automatically. Consequently, I missed Parm's two-in-the-morning phone call to my cell phone. She left a message, but grew impatient when I did not reply fast enough for her satisfaction.

218

Parm's Plan B was calling the house's landline number. I live in the basement of Logan's house. Actually it's Gerry's house, he bought it. And after a recent little flare-up with Logan's depression, Gerry moved into one of the upstairs bedrooms. Actually it has turned out a lot better than I expected. Logan, Gerry, and Wendy have become quite close. Gerry's great, he cooks, cleans, and keeps the house well stocked with fantastic food. We all get along fabulously. Gerry is the most easygoing guy around. He is going to be a grandfather and has become the happiest man in the neighbourhood. Logan is still weird, but he's working on his issues. He and Wendy went to dinner with his mother in Seattle last week.

I was sound asleep, level three or four, yet Gerry calling me from the upstairs doorway penetrated my consciousness. "Raj, your sister is on the telephone, she says it's important."

Put on my robe and stumbled up the stairs. "Sorry Gerry, hope my sister didn't wake you," I apologized.

"Oh no problem Raj, we're watching a movie upstairs," Gerry gestured. "I'm baking some cookies, but they're not ready yet. Couple more minutes to go."

The receiver of the black landline wall phone rested on the kitchen counter. I picked it up. "Hi Parm, what's up, why are you calling me so late and on the house landline?"

"You didn't answer your cell phone, that's why."

"I never answer late at night, you should have left a message."

"I did leave a message and you didn't reply."

Growing impatient I asked, "Parm, what do you want?"

"I need to show you something, but we can't talk about it over an unsecure phone line."

With a groan I asked, "Can't it wait until tomorrow morning?"

"No, don't think so, tomorrow is too far away. This is important. Start making some chai, Punjabi style, and we'll be there in fifteen minutes."

"Who is the *we* you are talking about?"

"CC, me and Edilma."

"Why the cadrè? Can't you just come by *yourself?*"

"No, CC found the footage, she has to come and annotate. Edilma is driving, and I'm project leader. Kelsey went home."

"Okay, I'll put some water on and start crushing cardamom."

First thing, tea notwithstanding, is to change out of my pajamas into something more suitable to see my sister and her crazy friends. Evidently Caitlyn Chan, but everyone calls her CC, found some footage and it is important that I see it *now*.

Okay, it's almost two-thirty in the morning and Gerry's announcing, "Cookies are ready!"

Some Nights are Long

"You don't have to attend every argument you are invited to."
~Parminder K. Gill

❧

My brother Raj is well disciplined. He's always been that way, goes to bed early, gets up early, doesn't eat junk food, very reliable, but when Caitlyn uncovered the footage of Shane, I knew Raj better see it straight away. Even though seeing the footage would be extremely upsetting. It looks bad.

When we got to Logan's Larch Street house the place was lit up brightly and buzzing with activity. Mr. Meyers, Logan's dad, evidently moved into the place. Raj lives in the basement because he and Pops are still feuding. Mr. Meyers is a lot friendlier than Logan. He answered the door when we arrived. "Hello Parminder." I was impressed he remembered my name! "Just baked some fresh cookies, Raj made chai, c'mon in, please."

I introduced Caitlyn and Edilma and they dove into the cookie platter. Raj sauntered over giving me a head tilting look and a half-hug. "So what's so earth shatteringly important to get me out of bed on a school night?"

"You don't go to school Raj. Remember, you quit."

"It's a week night and I didn't quit, just taking a break!" Scowling now, "Show me what you've got."

"Maybe we should go somewhere bit more private," I asked softly.

"No, Gerry's cool, whatever this is, he's cool."

Thinking to myself, "Okay Raj, so be it." Of course that type of tone always helps get attention.

Gerry jumps over and says, "Here let me clear off the table and give space to work."

Caitlyn gives me a nod, pulls out her laptop, plunks it on the table, and while still eating a cookie begins to explain the footage she is going to show. "So, okay Raj, you know we've been using facial recognition software, scouring CCTV cameras in the public and private sectors looking for Shane. Well, we found him. Here is how it goes: the cops arrested Shane while he was walking down Point Grey Road near the Lululemon bunker-house because he had blood on his clothes. Guess that's considered probable cause or something. Whatever, yet Trent McKinney's dead body was found in David Lam Park in Yaletown. Declan Downes died in the emergency ward of Vancouver General Hospital." Caitlyn took a sip of tea, paused and continued. "Okay, so ambulance privacy rules and everything getting in our way we were eventually able to find out that Declan was picked up near the Mini Cooper place on Hamilton Street. And that's where it happened." Striking the keyboard she said, "Here, see for yourself. Sorry, no audio, just video."

Right at that point Wendy and Logan stumble down the stairs. "Hi Parm," Wendy says coming in with a hug. "Thought I heard your voice down here. What's happening?"

Logan was wearing Snoopy slippers; he reached for a hot cookie, I said, "Nice slippers Logan."

"Glad you like them Miss Parmesan-cheese because your opinion is so important to me," Logan said with a sarcastic hand flip.

I looked over to Raj for guidance.

"Yes, yes, go ahead, no secrets here at Larch house. Right Gerry?"

Gerry sighed, "Logan we haven't seen the footage yet, however, it seems the girls have found some CCTV camera video of Shane."

"Shane?"

"Yes, Shane and the other two boys," Gerry looked at me. "Is that correct Parminder?"

"What two other boys?" Logan asked indignantly.

"Trent and Declan," Raj answered for me.

"Okay," Logan stepped forward. "Let's see it."

Caitlyn turned to me with a wondering glance. "Sure, go ahead," I said.

Caitlyn nodded her head and began speaking with a preface, "So you know how television broadcasters warn that the following images may offend some viewers - same thing here. Now I don't know Shane the same as some of you."

Logan interrupted, "Just push start, no preamble or warnings needed."

Myself, sorta thought Caitlyn's warning was warranted, but Logan he's a tough guy. Raj says he's like Cancer the Crab: hard on the outside soft and mushy inside. I've already seen the video a few times, maybe five now, and the first couple don't really count because we weren't sure who it was and what was happening in the footage. It is tough to watch.

Everyone crowded around the laptop and watched as the video starts with an Asian couple coming down Nelson Street and turning right onto Hamilton. Shane's about ten steps behind. The three of them turned to see Trent and Declan off to the side saying something with gestures. The Asian couple looks down while Shane catches up to them and yells something back to Trent and Declan. Shane motions for the couple to carry on and flips a finger to the boys. This seems to escalate the situation as the two boys now approach Shane. The one guy, who we later learn is Declan, pulls out a knife and points it at Shane. Shane punches Declan in the face, grabs the knife and fends off Trent. The scuffle continues with blows being thrown back and forth. Shane clearly stabs Declan a number of times. Declan is down and blood is oozing onto the sidewalk. Trent tries to get away and Shane chases after him. You can't see what happens next because they are now out of the camera's range. You can see Declan getting up to his feet and stumbling down the street.

"Oh shit," Logan cried out quite loud. "Did you see that? Shane just stabbed that guy, with his own knife!"

Although I knew this was going to be hard for Raj, I also knew that Raj had an inkling it was a possibility. Mummy ji makes me follow her rules, and rules for Raj are different because he is a boy. "Ma, that's not fair!" I would tell her.

Reading Raj's private writings were always wrong, and I'd never do that, however, *eavesdropping,* is a different deal. I overheard Raj on the phone talking to Ned saying, "I don't know, sometimes I think he might have done it." I couldn't hear Ned's end of the convo, but I gathered Ned did not want to talk in that direction and Raj should drop it.

The *diffusion effect* was something our professor Caroline Harrell was talking about last week in our social psych class. Turns out to be a big help tonight. Watching the video all by himself would have been harder for Raj. Having all these people here help keep him calm. Logan, he's another story altogether.

Gerry jumps up and starts to take control. "Alright, I'm not a lawyer, but clearly, self-defense, it was self-defense. Who else has seen this film?"

"Other than the people here, Kelsey's seen it," I replied.

"Who is Kelsey?"

"Kelsey Weiss, she's part of our group. Raj hired her." I explained, "She was tired and went home. School night Raj."

Caitlyn pulled out a zip drive key. "This is the only copy. To whom should I give this drive?"

Raj holds out his hand, "Just give it to me. I'll handle it."

Edilma doesn't say too much at the best of times, yet she thought Raj should know: "If we could get this stuff you know it's likely only a matter of time until someone else gets it, too."

"Thanks, yes, I understand."

"Thanks for the cookies Mr. Meyers." I gave him a thumb up signal. "We've got to get going, school tomorrow."

Gerry said, "Yes, yes, of course, I will walk you to the door."

We collected our stuff, Caitlyn took another cookie for the road and we left. "Good night Raj."

"Night Parm." He gave me another half-hug. "Thanks, you did good work."

Amelia's Sunrise Too Soon

"There is no right way to do a wrong thing." ~Amelia Reilly

❧

Raj has been a positive person in my life. He's been helpful in so many ways; don't know what I'd do without him. Thanks to Raj I've started to kick some bad habits, modify others. Started eating better, certainly started sleeping better. Didn't really think that much about sleep hygiene until Raj emphasized, "You can't have a good *day* unless you have a good *night*." Sleep is important to Raj. Sometimes, in the middle of the night, if I thought of something I'd go write it down, check messages or data processing progress. That stuff freaks Raj out.

Raj explains, "Neurologically speaking, if you turn on a light in the middle of the night you interrupt the sleep cycle and jolt the cerebral cortex to a higher processing level than what it should be!" Sometimes Raj will get up in the middle of the night to go pee, but no lights needed. He tiptoes back and forth in the dark—eyes like a cat.

All devices get turned off or to do not disturb mode. He's okay with my cell phone on the nightstand, but the ringer must be OFF. Can't argue, he's correct and I've been feeling better, more productive and happier following his simple sleep suggestions. Happier just having Raj around.

Actually, I've known Raj for years. He's one of Ned's best friends. Yet I never really *knew* him until he returned from India for Shane's trial. Guess because Raj is three years younger it made more a difference years gone by. Or, maybe we've both just matured. Either way it's been wonderful having Raj around.

Sometimes I sleep in my office. I don't think it's as big a deal as some others, who make like it is an academic administrative faux pas. And it's not like I'm booking in eight to ten hours of sleep. And I don't do it all the time. I've got a cot that folds down to a bed and sometimes if I just lay down for a few hours, maybe three to four, I wake up rejuvenated. Rather than drive home, sleeping in the office works well.

Following Raj's rules for adequate sleep hygiene, I set my phone down, close by, with the ringer off. I cover my eyes with a sleep mask and use the Shane Bighill auditory sleep approach by putting airpods in my ears playing soothing tunes. Nowadays, while sleeping I never check messages, nor send any either. Raj says, "Morning comes soon enough to deal with those things."

So, last night I was working late in the office, started to feel fatigued and decided to fold out the cot and sleep for a few hours. Morning arrived too soon and I woke up with a long line of messages from Raj, my mother, Uncle R, Nina, Dr. Quan and some others that I'll deal with later.

Raj had sent a text message at 3:30 and voice mail at four: "Please call me ASAP it is important." I called him back but got his message, "Hi Raj, it's 6:30 and I'm sure you are still sleeping. We're playing telephone tag. Call me when you can."

Uncle R left a text message saying, "Sent you an email." That's deep and cryptic, why use two modes when one would suffice. Nevertheless, I checked my email and his read, "Please let me know when I can come and see you. It is important."

I can't call any of his numbers at 6:30 in the morning so I simply replied to the email saying, "Up at UBC. You can come up to my office anytime this morning or I could come to yours in the afternoon?"

The phone shows my mum called a half dozen times, left two text messages and one email. The first text message in capital letters read: "WHERE ARE YOU? CALL ME ASAP" and the second in lowercase letters read, "call me it is important."

Shaking my head, talking to myself, all I could think was, "Whew, I go to sleep for a few hours and the world falls apart." Although everyone wants an immediate response, it's still too early in the morning, and I already left Raj a message. Might as well call my mum. Got her on speed dial and my new cell will let me call all her private numbers and landline simultaneously. I pushed the button and don't think I even heard a ring tone before she picks up crying, "Amelia, Jedd's dead!"

"Okay."

"No it's not okay!" she shrieks back at me. "Where are you?"

"UBC." I didn't know what else to say other than, "I'm on my way right away. See you soon."

"Okay."

Pulled myself together and got home as quickly as I could. It took twenty minutes tops. I came flying through the front doors, but mum was nowhere to be seen, and I figured she must be upstairs. As I have done for the last twenty-five years, I yelled, "I'm home." Heard the toilet flushing, water running, and she emerged.

"Thank god you are here," she said softly.

I gave her a big hug and asked, "What happened?"

"Jedd stroked out, his heart stopped, and they were unable to revive him. He died."

"Someone called you?"

"Yes, some resident flunky left me a cryptic message for me to call the hospital. When I called that guy was gone and I got the twenty-four hour on-call intern help line. I had to bully him into telling me what was going on. He caved when he noted that I was listed as legal counsel on Jedd's disclosure form. His ex-wife, Maureen McAllister, is listed as the family contact."

"Didn't know he was married."

She sighed, and said, "He is and he isn't. They have been separated for over twenty years with a legal separation agreement. However, they never divorced officially because Maureen is a Catholic and devout Catholics do not get divorced."

"Wow, oh wow," I snorted. "Did you know any of this?"

"Yes, but at the time it didn't seem to matter to Jedd. And it certainly wasn't any of my business. Ours was a casual relationship in its infancy."

"Maureen is making funeral arrangements," she sighed. "I got an email with some information and directives."

"An email?"

"Yes, she's planning a large funeral at the Christ Church downtown at Burrard and Georgia Streets. Open casket and Catholic ceremonial prayers and procedures. The whole thing."

A Witness Came Forward

Parry Sound's Bobby Orr knew a lot about winning, yet he said, "There are no environments where you're only going to win, because life is just not like that."

⁂

I met with Brent Farrow first thing Tuesday morning at the York Avenue Psychology office. Although I made like I was really busy, it would be unprofessional not to see Brent sooner rather than later.

Unquestionably, Brent presents with a long list of problems that he was hoping I could help alleviate and maybe even extinguish. At the initial clinical interview we discussed how to develop some psychotherapy goals and objectives. I explained Cognitive Behavioural Therapy (CBT) basics in relation to PTSD treatment.

"Is that kid with the red hair your patient?" Brent asked almost out of the blue. "I know shrinks aren't supposed to talk about their patients, but I was wondering."

Although this wasn't a conversation I wanted, I replied, "Shane Bighill?"

"Yeah, I saw him do it. He killed those guys that were saying racist shit to the Chinese people. I was there, I saw it happen."

Later that day when Raj showed us the footage projected onto Annette's big screen television, usually commandeered by Ned, it was quite clear to see Brent in the background shadows smoking a cigarette. He had been out cavorting with his friends and stopped for a smoke before going over to his girlfriend's apartment for a late night rendezvous. She won't let him smoke inside or even on the balcony anymore. It has become big issue between them.

Brent understood the psychologist and patient ethical rules of confidentiality. He knew I could not tell anyone the things he told me in session. However, he made it clear that after lunch today he was accompanying his girlfriend to the police department to report what he saw the night of the murders.

Once I knew Brent had made his report to the police, I made efforts to eventually get a hold of Amelia. She was consoling Annette, who was quite inconsolable due to Jedd's sudden death.

Raj also was trying to track down Amelia and Annette so they could view the CCTV camera footage.

As difficult days go, this was one of the worst for everyone. Likely to become more difficult as we moved forward.

Amelia turned to me, did some sighs and head nods. "Well, we'll just have to go one day at a time, I guess."

"Yes, let's do that." Annette's voiced croaked and wavered. "I've got funeral stuff to deal with tomorrow. It's an open casket event."

Amelia made a grimacing face, "Open casket, eh?"

Annette nodded, "Yes."

Goodbye My Friend

Before Parkinsons stole Linda Ronstadt's singing voice she sang, "Oh we never know where life will take us. I know it's just a ride on the wheel. And we never know when death will shake us. And we wonder how it will feel. Goodbye my friend, I know I'll never see you again, but it's okay, Goodbye my friend." From the album *Cry Like a Rainstorm, Howl Like the Wind* (1989). Karla Bonoff wrote the lyrics to *Goodbye my Friend.*

※

Again, over a poor phone line connection, Nina assured me, "Ned, don't worry we won't be late."

"Okay, but Shane's *always* late," I moaned.

Nina replied, "Ned, remember worry is a waste of imagination."

"I'm not worried, Shane's always late, and it's an empirical fact."

So of course Nina and Shane ended up running late. While we were waiting for them outside the Christ Church Cathedral in downtown Vancouver, I was trying to explain the anthropological significance of Catholic funerals to Raj, Logan and Wendy when this big guy with a walrus moustache comes forward, sticks his hand out to shake and says, "Hello lads, how you doing?"

Logan looks at him with squinty eyes, "Do we know you?"

"Well, gents, we met a long time ago," the big guy smiled. "I'm Captain Norm DuPont from the Gibsons Volunteer Fire Department."

Logan dove towards him and hugged him hard, "I remember you." Logan started getting weepy. "You're the guy who cut Banny down from the tree."

"Yes, well, we were there to help with the coroner's office."

Almost on cue Nina rolls up in the Mercedes van with Shane and Harpreet. She beep beeps the horn so we will help unload Harry.

Logan takes the firefighter by the arm and says, "C'mon, you need to see Harry."

Shane slides open the van's door, "What's up buttercup?"

"Shane, this is Captain DuPont!"

"Okay," Shane wiggled his face, and saluted.

"We met him all those years ago at Camp Byng." Logan caught his breath. "He took care of Banny."

Harpreet's hearing is overcompensatingly good, mostly because he can't talk, I guess. He came rolling out of the van eager to meet the firefighter. "Hello sir," his voice synthesizer said, "I am pleased to meet you. Thank you for your service."

Captain Norm smiled, "Nice to meet you too, son. Glad to see you doing so well. Nice wheels."

"Are you related to Mr. Talbot?" I asked.

"No, no, I'm not," Captain Norm shook his head. "Mr. Talbot has a cottage on the water just outside Roberts Creek and he was always a big supporter of our fire department. I'm here to pay respects. Seeing you lads today is an added bonus."

My mum and Uncle R were walking towards us, I could see she was a little worse for wear. "We better take our seats," Uncle R suggested.

"We have seats?" Shane asked. "Thought they were called pews?"

"Yes, Angela has a section set aside for us with a suitable space for Harry," Uncle R gestured to the entrance. "Lets go inside."

The cathedral was packed. Evidently, Jedd Talbot was well known by so many. When we reached the door Angela appointed a young lady to escort us to our section of pews. Amelia was already inside, sitting by herself.

The Rule of Law

"Where were you when it didn't happen?" ~Amelia Jean Reilly

꙰

I arrived at the church early. "Hello Amelia," Angela gave me a hug. "The service won't start for a while." She had a section set aside so our group could all sit together. The whole atmosphere was so sad, somber, and I tried ever so hard not to constantly cry. I didn't want to cry over Jedd, or Shane, and I didn't want to cry because I knew Raj was making plans to return to India. It was all just so sad.

Raj held my hand throughout the funeral service. Neither of us really knew what was going on most of the time. Raj is a Sikh and this was the first Catholic funeral I've attended. Lots of prayers, kneeling, eulogies and hymns intermingled with the priest's speech and sermon seemed to go on forever. And then it ended, everyone filed outside and we stood on the sidewalk with a strong afternoon blinding sun. Sunglasses, thank god, helped my bloodshot eyes and me while we were shaking hands and sharing hugs with various well wishers. My mum was a mess.

Uncle R leaned over and whispered in my ear, "I'm going to take your mother home now. Don't think she needs to go to the wake."

Nodding my head, I agreed, "Yes, good idea."

Earlier in the morning I overheard Ned explaining the rule of law to Logan and Wendy through the speaker of his cell phone. They were alarmed and worried about what was going to happen now that an eyewitness had come forward. What would happen now that the video has surfaced? Ned, who explains everything from an "anthropological perspective" didn't seem to diminish their fears.

Logan wanted to know, "What's the difference between manslaughter and second-degree murder?"

"Is that something the judge and jury decides?" Wendy asked. "Or will the crown prosecutor make a plea bargain deal?"

"What about self-defense? My dad says Shane will get off because it was clearly self-defense."

Wendy snorted, "Logan, your father is a stockbroker. He doesn't know anything about the judicial system and homicides."

Logan made a moaning noise, "I guess, but he knows more than I do. What do you think Ned?"

Yes, as an unauthorized eavesdropper, I also wanted to hear Ned's response to their questions. However, their speaker phone conference call came to a screeching halt with Ned saying, "Sorry, Logan, gotta go, Nina's calling on my call waiting screen. We are working on transportation logistics."

Hardball and Hindsight

Ursula Jardine and I go way back. We went to law school together, afterwards we both clerked at the BC Supreme Court, and we were called to the bar at the same time. Now Amelia and I are sitting outside her office waiting for a meeting. Our career paths travelled in different directions. Until recently, most of my legal work was in civil law. The corporate domain has been good to me. Ursula, on the other hand, is now the Senior Crown Prosecutor for the lower mainland district region.

"Making us wait is a power play," Amelia scoffed. "They're trying to ice us."

"No, I don't see it that way, dear," I tried to placate her. "This is a busy office and ours is not the only file needing attention today."

Reluctantly, during the drive downtown, Amelia agreed that I would lead our side of the conversation and do *all* the talking with the crown prosecutors. Amelia was to respond *only* if it was essential and *helpful* to the case. We would keep our emotions in check. Amelia's job was to take notes and observe.

Finally, some teenager, must be an intern, came out of the frosted conference room door and invited us inside. Ursula and two junior prosecutors sat on one side of the table, Amelia and I on the other.

"Thanks for meeting with us this morning Ursula," I said with a smile.

"Yes, Ms. Reilly, of course our office is always happy to oblige your request for a meeting," she said somewhat flatly. "How can I help you?"

"Thought this might be a good time for us to meet and discuss a revised plea to present to the judge." I kept my smile and pleasantries front and centre.

"Very well," Ursula replied. "You now wish to enter a guilty plea?"

"No," my smile faded. "Given the emerging evidence I did not think you would wish to continue with a second degree murder charge."

"Oh, well, of course," she shook her head, "We still do not feel that Mr. Bighill held any premeditation and a charge of first degree would not be appropriate."

"We were thinking self-defense."

Ursula gave me a smug sort of grimace. "We see it differently, and the eye-witness testimony will not support self-defense."

"How so?"

She opened a file, pulled out a piece of paper and slid it across the table. "Certainly, in your cross-examination you may ask the witness for further details. However, as you can see in the affidavit our witness will testify that Mr. Bighill stabbed Mr. Downes." Additionally, he pursued Mr. McKinney down the street screaming: "*You are going to die racist motherfucker!*" Mr. Bighill tracked him down and murdered Mr. McKinney. Ursula shook her head. "The evidence clearly does not support a claim of self-defense."

I looked her square in the eye and said, "We see it differently."

"Very well then," she got up, stuck out her hand to shake mine, "see you in court."

Brought my faux smile back, stood up, shook her hand and said, "See you in court."

I nodded to Amelia. We walked out briskly, got in the elevator, and Amelia turned me and said, "We're screwed, eh."

"No, no, not at all," I tried to reassure her. "She's just doing her job. I expect a call later today or tomorrow. They're not going to pursue a second degree charge."

"Really," Amelia sneered, "I didn't hear any indication they would entertain a self-defense plea bargain!"

"Maybe not right now," I agreed, "but this is far from over at this point."

"Really?"

"Really."

The elevator stopped on the ninth floor, a trio of lawyers entered and we moved to the back corner. "Want me to drop you off at UBC?" I asked Amelia.

"No, thanks," she pursed her lips, "I have to go and see Nina and Shane."

Amelia ~
Crocodiles Are Not Friendly

Steve Irwin, an Australian nature expert, nicknamed The Crocodile Hunter, explained, "Crocs are easy to understand. They try to kill and eat you. People are harder. Sometimes they pretend to be your friend first." (Steve Irwin, 1962 – 2006).

It was a difficult morning. We met with the Senior Crown Prosecutor and her team to try and reach an out of court settlement. There were strange dynamics between my mother and Ursula Jardine that went well beyond my understanding. Lawyer games, I guess, but sure seemed to me as though we struck out when the meeting ended, awkwardly. Mum was more optimistic than me. "Show some patience," she said with more confidence than I'd expect. The art of out-lawyering the other side is not my forté.

Nina was working from home and pretending as though she wasn't anxiously waiting for me to arrive and tell her the morning's news. When I got there their townhouse was unusually quiet. "Hi, how you doing?" with a full hug. "Where's Shane?"

"Bike riding with his buddies."

"Great," I smiled. "Good to get him out doing something productive."

Nina smiled, "Yes, good to get him out, period." Holding out her palms, "How did it go this morning? What's the deal?"

"No deal," I said shaking my head. "Ursula Jardine, the Crown Prosecutor seems to think a charge of second degree murder floats well enough to convince the jury. My mum thinks otherwise."

"Self-defense?"

"No luck on that count," I commented with a sigh. "Maybe manslaughter."

"What does that mean?"

"Don't really know other than it's way better than second degree murder."

Nina was feeling weathered from all the unfolding events. Shortly after Raj had given me a copy of the video I had taken it over to show Nina. It was a tough time. First we watched together and then it got worse when we called Shane in to watch it. He reacted with a resigned sort of sadness. "Guess this shows I did it. I really didn't know if I did or not. I was too wasted to remember," he grimaced. "Video only shows the one guy, what about the other one?"

I had to tell them about the eyewitness. "Yes, the CCTV camera only captures you and Declan Downes. The witness says you chased Trent McKinney, caught him and stabbed him."

"Yes, I believe him," Shane said softly. "That's likely what happened. Sorry Nina, I fucked up. Can't take it back but wish I could."

Nina started crying. Shane tried to give her a hug, but she pushed him away. "What happens now, Amelia?"

"Don't know yet," I explained. "We've asked for a meeting with the Crown Prosecutor and I'll know more after that."

All my life Uncle R says, "Don't make promises you cannot keep!" So now here I am drinking tea with Nina after the meeting with the crown attorneys and with nothing productive to say. I thought,

"Good thing Shane is out bike riding with his buddies. Wish I hadn't promised to know more than I do. Wish this wasn't what it is."

The factual truth is that Shane ended the lives of two people. That much we now know for certain. The legal theatre remains to be seen. Certainly, the video clearly shows self-defense with Declan Downes. There is no doubt there. Any jury watching the video would have to agree that was self-defense. However, the eyewitness is going to testify that Shane chased Trent McKinney down with a threat to kill him. The crown says that shows *intent* to kill with *malice*. My mum says self-defense still applies because Trent threatened Shane in the first instance observed at the beginning of the video.

I'm not much of a gambler. I'm a whiz with mathematical probability theory. Settling out of court would have been better. No other algorithm can help here. It's always a roll of the dice with a jury. Who knows how twelve people are going to see the facts?

Just received a text message from mum: "CALL OR COME OVER ASAP."

Ned ~
Justice, the Truth, and Laws

"Psychometrically, hearing and listening are not orthogonal. They are different, more likely oblique." ~Dr. Bruno Zumbo, University of British Columbia, Distinguished Scholar

It was a perfect day for bike riding. Not too hot, not too cold, and it had rained a couple of days ago so the UBC endowment trails weren't dusty or muddy. Getting dirty is okay, and expected, but last year I wiped out in the slippery mud and that really sucked. Bent my front tyre rim, forks, and got hurt, too. Shane tried to console me, "No broken bones or stitches needed for your pretty face."

"Fuck off Shane."

"Hey, hey, hey," he pleaded, "sorry, no hostilities needed."

Today just before lunch we were blasting single file through the woods down the trail that ends up at the Spanish Banks West Concession Stand. We always stop to say bonjour to the proprietors, André, and his lovely wife Lise Bourbonnais, retired teachers from Quebec City. They've run this hotdog stand as long as I can remember. I love to listen to the Bourbonnais bicker while they work. They are a loving couple for sure. We always get poutine, fish and chips, and milk shakes. I love to eat on the picnic tables that have a view to the west of the Salish Sea and Lighthouse Park on the other side.

Logan called Wendy to check in and let her know where he was because she likes that and he's behaving better. Everybody else pulled out their devices to check number of kilometres travelled, messages, and the state of the real world.

My cell screen had a message from mum in all caps saying: CALL OR COME OVER ASAP. She has learned how to do simultaneous group messages and I could see my sister, Uncle R and Angela's names on the list. Before calling mum I of course called Amelia. She never picks up anymore and I went directly to voicemail. "Namaste Amelia, it's Ned calling. We got a message from Mum. What's the deal, butane needed?"

Butane needed is our old code for whether or not mum was lighting her hair on fire unnecessarily. Amelia started it.

Just when I was starting to put my cell away it began to vibrate, Amelia was *calling* me. She never calls. Usually an instant message is her mode.

"Namaste Amelia, what's up?"

"Am I on speaker?"

"No, do you want to be?"

"NO!" she said emphatically. "This is private."

"Okay," Amelia had my attention. "Is this about Mum? I got her text." I got up and walked away from earshot of the guys. They were all involved with eating, and electronics. They didn't care about me and whatever I was doing anyway.

"Can you talk?" Amelia asked.

"Yes, shoot."

"Mum's on top of her game. She's a phenomenal lawyer."

"Okay." Amelia seldom speaks so complimentary about our mother.

"No, really, she is," Amelia moaned. "Remember when I thought I was so hot? Well, I was not. It was Jedd. He made like I was a rising star. I've been over my head for a while now."

"What's going on? Should I call her or go over?" I asked.

"No, there's nothing for you to do. She's just keeping you in the loop. Mostly she wanted to bounce ideas off Uncle R and me."

"Like what?"

"The other side is playing hardball and she's holding her own."

"The other side?"

"Yes, the Senior Crown Prosecutor and her team are playing lawyer games."

"How so?"

"We met this morning to see if we could settle out of court. They're playing hardball saying their witness will testify that Shane acted with malice and intent to kill. So second degree murder is what they are prepared to present to the jury."

"What about self-defense?"

"Yes, agreed, that's what I thought. Declan and Trent threatened Shane in the first instance with the knife, but Shane took the knife, stabbed Declan, and chased Trent down saying he'd kill him, *according to the witness.*"

"What about the video? It shows Shane taking the knife and stabbing one guy, but we didn't see a chase scene. Is that good or bad?"

"Dunno, the witness is what they are relying on rather than the video."

"Hey Amelia, I should get going here. The guys are getting restless and we've got the Highbury Hill to climb next."

"Okay, stay in touch."

"Dinner?"

"Yes, see you at dinner."

"Hey, Amelia."

"Yes?"

"Thanks."

"Too soon for offering thank yous, we've got a couple of hills to climb at this end."

Shane Says Que Sera, Sera

Oscar nominee for *The Big Chill,* and *Grand Canyon,* director of *Dreamcatcher,* co-writer of *The Empire Strikes Back* and *Raiders of the Lost Ark,* Lawrence Kasdan, explains, "Tomorrow is a day different than today."

❧

Yesterday we had a great day! The guys took me out bike riding through the UBC trails; lunch at our favourite hotdog stand on the beach, and Logan's dad did an elaborate barbeque dinner for all our friends. It was terrific! A top shelf day for sure.

Earlier I had a feeling things were brewing on the legal front when Ned started acting weirdish while we were at the hotdog stand. He took a phone call from someone and danced around on the spot out of earshot. I asked him if everything was copacetic and he said, "Worry is a waste of imagination. Let's hit the Highbury Street hill!" I love biking up that hill. It's one of the best in town. A tough climb, but a tonne of fun to see who can crest the top first.

Logan's dad did a big turnabout a while back. He and Logan are tight of tightest these days. They used to squabble about everything and anything. Nowadays they're all buddy buddy and smiles all the time. Of course, Wendy's pregnancy seems to make a difference. Seriously, Logan's dad has really become a great guy. He's uber nice to all of us.

Ned and me were standing by the hot tub when Logan's dad came by with a tray of ice-cold beers. "Might I interest you two in more ribs, another burger or a cold beer?"

"No, thanks Gerry," Ned held up his palms. "I'm stuffed, we gotta shove off and go to a meeting."

"We do?" I asked.

"Yeah, I promised my mum that we'd go over and talk to her after dinner."

"And who is the *we* you are talking about?"

Ned shrugged, looked around, and side kicked at the grass, "Well, at minimum, you, me and Nina have to go. We don't need to shift the whole party over."

"It's bad news, right."

"I don't know much," Ned looked me in the eyes and then downward. "Really I don't know much, but we don't want to smell like beer because she will get weird. She'll do the drinking and driving sermon."

"We'll take the bikes," I suggested.

Ned looked like he's gonna start crying, "Let's just get in the car and go, okay?" He nodded at me.

"Yes, hey buddy, we're good here. No worries, whenever, and wherever you want to go I'm right beside you. You can count on me." I didn't want Ned to squirm or feel bad about anything. It had been a great day. Of course, we can go *talk* to his mum. She's carrying a lot of the load now that my main lawyer Jedd T died. He was a good guy. I liked him a lot. All this courtroom legal beagle mumbo jumbo's stressing everyone out. Jedd didn't get stressed, but he's gone, we're carrying on—one way or another.

Ned waved to my sister, who was deep in discussion with Parminder's gang. They shared a round of hugs and Nina came trotting over. "Time to go?" she asked.

"Yup," Ned looked over at me, "changed my mind, you want to go by bikes Shane?"

"Always," I said with a smile.

Nina slugged me on the shoulder, "Fine, I'll go by car with Amelia. Raj asked if he could come, too. I said yes."

"Yeah, for sure, he's the best. See you there sis." With a royal wave to the gang, Ned and I took off on the bikes. We flew full speed all the way and beat the car folks by ten minutes. Of course, some time gets credited to their weak disengaging skills.

"Remember when Logan said never go into a place where there are more than three cars in the driveway because it's likely an intervention?"

"Yeah, Logan knows this sort of stuff, eh?" Ned smiled.

"Remember Raj, Wendy and Logan's dad did an intervention on him?"

"Yeah, that worked well," Ned said while we locked the bikes in the garage.

Uncle R and his wife Harjit were already there via the old red bug-eyed sports car. Didn't know before, but Angela drove a pickup truck. I don't know who else was there; it didn't matter because I knew they were all there supporting me.

We walked inside and were immediately hit with nice aromatic smells of tapas and hors d'oeuvres. Ned turned to me with a smile, "Good news, more food. Biking recovered my appetite."

Folks were milling about with some in the kitchen and others on the back deck. Ned's mum rushed towards us with big hugs and slobbering cheek kisses. "How was dinner?" she asked. "I hope you saved room for dessert."

"Of course," I patted my tummy, "always room for dessert."

Amelia, Raj and Nina came bursting through the door with Amelia complaining, "Oh gawd, not more food."

"No probs Amelia," Ned said, "more for us. Right Shane."

I could tell the pleasantries and small talks were coming to a close when Uncle R came into the room saying, "Oh good, everyone's here, shall we sit at the dining room table for a discussion?"

Ned and Raj moved in a couple of extra chairs and everyone crowded around the table. Nina broke the ice saying, "Just want to start off by saying thank you Mrs. Reilly, for having us over to your home. This is much more comfortable than the sterile conference room at the law firm. Shane and I appreciate all of your tireless work. I don't know where we'd be without you. Right Shane?" she says while patting me on the shoulder.

I sat up straight. "Yes, yes," I agreed whole heartedly. "Thanks for everything."

She got started by saying the crown prosecutor's office was originally taking a tough stance and were sticking to the original charge of second-degree murder. I killed two people and that is a fact. It can't be spun into an *alternative fact* the way politicos spin stuff. She stopped for a second, took a swig of her tea, and shook her head. "I told them the video evidence clearly shows self-defense. However, they disagreed and continue to feel their eye witness supports the charge of second degree."

Amelia jumped in, "And is this witness reliable?"

With an eye roll dynamic I didn't understand, "We've been over this, yes, the witness' reliability is not an issue."

Then she looked at me and described her post-meeting phone call from the senior crown prosecutor. In order to spare the McKinney and Downes' families a painful protracted trial, the crown reconsidered would agree to a reduced charge of manslaughter. I had seen the parents in the courthouse. They were mad at each other thinking the other kid led their kid astray. Nobody *wins* these things.

"Manslaughter," Amelia scoffed, "really."

Uncle R stepped in, "Amelia," he pleaded, "let your mother finish."

"No, it's fine. I am finished," she said. "They are waiting to hear back from me. I explained that I would bring their deal to Shane and Nina. And in due course, I'd get back to them."

Nina twitched and sighed, "So, what does this mean? Where are we now?"

As I have learned throughout this legal process, the answer is never simple. It's the old adage where a bird in the hand is better than two in the bush. An agreement is better for both sides because neither want to lose and who knows what verdict the jury might render. We could continue with self-defense and the crown could go with second degree. If the jury believes that I killed Trent and Declan out of self-defense, we win, I go free, case dismissed. If the jury believes I unlawfully killed with intent and malice then its second degree and I go to jail for a long time. Mind you, manslaughter or second degree, either way I'm going to jail.

Nina looked at me, "What do you think?"

What could I tell her? I didn't know what to say anymore. I seriously was sorry for the whole thing. If I could turn back time of course I would not have killed those guys. It was a time in my life when I was a complete asshole, always wasted and acting stupid. Wish I was a better person, but I did do it. I killed them. "Don't know Nina, but I think we should take the deal, eh?" Pursed my lips and grimaced. "Wish dad were here, he'd know what to do."

Nina nodded, "Yes, he'd know what to do."

Uncle R jumped back in to the convo, "Well, Annette," he waved his hand, "a decision does not need to be delivered today, right?"

"No, of course not, but the crown would like to file a joint submission to the judge tomorrow morning."

"What about sentencing?" Amelia asked, probably louder than needed.

Harjit, Ned's aunt, who had sat quietly listening throughout the discussion, explained. "Amelia, I'm just here having a cup of tea with my family, even so, I can tell you sentencing will not happen tomorrow. The judge must consider the submission's merits. Sentencing is another issue."

"I knew that," Amelia was quick to reply.

We all smiled. It was helpful to see Amelia blush. "Okay," I looked around the table, "yes, tell them I agree to manslaughter. It is what is." I looked over at Ned, "We gotta go let Logan know."

"We could call."

"Naw gotta do it face-to-face."

I got up, gave Nina a pat on the shoulder, "Thank you everyone, you are the best friends in the world. Thanks for everything." I didn't want to do a round of hugs, kisses or anything, so just turned and walked out. I needed to let Logan and Raj know what's happening. And I needed some fresh air, too. "Meet you outside, Ned."

I stood outside on the front lawn taking in a couple of deep breaths, thought about Harpreet. Gotta talk to him soon. Logan will not take this well. He's bad that way. Just then Raj and Ned come thundering out the front door, Ned yells, "C'mon Shane, we're driving. I got the keys to Amelia's mighty Mini."

Banny's Boys

"Just because you can't help everyone, doesn't man you shouldn't help everyone you can." ~Captain (ret) N.P.C. Zimmer

❧

Although everyone knows it does not rain every day in Vancouver, it does seem to rain everyday when Shane appears in court. And although my sister says she is not superstitious, I know she is. We're all going to court today for Shane's sentencing. Thus, we travel cavalcade, same formation as we took ten days ago when Shane's manslaughter plea was entered into the court's record.

I thought we would be early arrivals to the courtroom. Not so, the place was packed. The mood was somber and ever so serious. Ned, Raj and Logan always sit in the third row. It's their lucky courtroom row. Superstitions are contagious.

Everyone stands when Judge Wallace enters the courtroom. She sits down, and begins to describe the history of the case, the evidence, victim impact statements, and Shane's criminal record. She sentenced Shane to four years in prison. An audible gasp rang through the courtroom, followed by tears and sobbing as the sheriffs placed handcuffs on Shane and led him away to begin serving his sentence.

Harpreet has a horn on his wheelchair. When the sentence was read out to the courtroom he started honking the chair's horn incessantly. The horn is really loud. The noise from the chair kept sounding until Wendy was able to disconnect it and shut it off.

A few of Shane's friends shouted some words of encouragement as he disappeared through the side courtroom door. The rest of the room began to disperse and everyone went their respective ways. Annette said she needed some alone time. She had hoped for a much lighter sentence, "That's the way the law works."

I drove home by myself. The whole time I thought, "Uh oh Randal, this was not what we expected."

Epilogue

The same day Shane was put in prison my nephew Ned moved in with Nina under the auspices of "We don't want Nina to be alone now that Shane is gone. The place is empty without him."

Of course my sister took the news poorly, "They are too young to live together. What if Nina gets pregnant? What will happen then?"

"We will celebrate," I said cheerfully, "a grandchild would be a gift!"

I knew Nina was not going to get pregnant. She is a twenty-three year old scientist, but if she did, I'd be happy. My sister sees catastrophes too easily. Her glass is always half-empty. Annette is a belt and suspenders lawyer. Nothing is left to chance. Things could go easier, yet this is how it is and I know she'll be fine. Lawyers look at life differently.

With a four-year sentence Shane was shipped off to a Federal Penitentiary in the Fraser Valley just outside Abbotsford. We were able to visit in groups of four fairly easily. Harpreet was problematic because once we got him inside it was impossible to get him to leave. He'd shutdown his chair, immobilizing it so it could not be moved. Shane started crying as the guards took him back to the cells.

The boys started counting down how many days Shane had left to serve. Generally, a four-year sentence would translate into thirty-two months with one-third of the sentence reduced for *good behaviour.* Gramps always said, "Don't count your chickens before they hatch."

Some sort of misperception or miscommunication led Shane to head-butt a couple of restraining prison guards, which took away the good behaviour clause and added another year to his sentence. He was transferred to a maximum-security prison outside Regina, Saskatchewan. This meant the drive took us longer. It involved a one-week each month's excursion. Gerry Meyers covered the costs and did all the organizing. He was a big help. When winter arrived with all the snow driving was impassable and Gerry arranged for us to fly once a month.

Gerry had a customized coach house built for Harpreet behind the house where he, Logan and Wendy lived. Although Gerry is an accomplished negotiator he took Ned and me with him to coax the Dhaliwals consent. "It would be a good thing for both Logan and Harpreet if they could live closer to each other. The coach house would be an ideal solution."

Harpreet's parents were given a key to the coach house and encouraged to visit whenever they wished. Harpreet and Logan were happy with the new living arrangements. Wendy was happy, too. The three of them began attending prenatal coaching classes. Logan called it "pre-noodle school."

Raj moved back to the Punjab University in Chandigarh to complete his studies. His father was pleased to see him return to university, but Amelia was not. They had grown quite close and she missed him something awful.

Amelia went to visit Raj. She lasted two weeks, and returned suffering from a culture crisis. India was difficult for Amelia. Her language skills were adequate yet culturally she struggled. "Things work differently in India," Raj tried to explain.

Although there are always lots of cars continually honking horns, the traffic is often terrifying. Raj rides around on an old Royal Enfield motorbike. All his friends do the same thing. He tried explaining to Amelia that the Indian young ladies ride on the back of the bikes all covered up in a headscarf type of burka or veil because of the dust, but also to ensure no one knows who is on the back of the bike. Anonymity is a good thing with nosy neighbours. This did not sit well with Amelia. Neither did many of the other somewhat *sexist* Indian traditions. "Amelia, things are different here, political correctness and culture are relative."

After Amelia returned to Vancouver she realized how much she cared for Raj. She was miserable without him. She got her UBC research endowment finances in a row and managed to transfer funds to the Punjab University. She went back to India to be with Raj. Amelia could carry on some of her research work from overseas. So far, so good, time will tell how things work out. Like it or not, Amelia has some of her mother's personality traits. I love them both, but rolling rocks uphill can be difficult.

Logan and Ned cut a digital EP with Thomas and the New Mahjeeroms. *Oxford Comma* came out as an unplugged acoustic tune and a jazzed-up electric tune. Amazingly, the way the music business works, the *Oxford Comma* went viral. Royalties are rolling in by the boatload. Ned, however, promised his mother university is his first priority. He will graduate. Music is only a hobby, at this point.

In Canada, does not matter whether you are County Court Circuit Judge, Queens Bench, or Supreme Court, all judges at all levels mandatory retirement occurs at age seventy-five. Hence, Harjit has some years to go and seems to still enjoy her job. Retirement appears as a horizon issue for her.

Myself, working, as a psychotherapist has been a rewarding career, still I sometimes think about retiring. Maybe I'll do it slowly, in stages or something. It was time consuming and difficult to obtain the psychologist's license, so it is hard to know when to give it up and not practice anymore. Still, I'd like to spend more time at the sea shack watching the tides ebb and flow. High tide is my favourite. It is easier to launch the kayak at high tide.

Last week Wendy gave birth to an eight pound, five ounce baby girl. They named her Banny Orton Meyers. She is a sweetheart.

Acknowledgements

The late great Richard Wagamese wrote in his novel *Indian Horse*, "It's not easy bringing a book into this world." Richard was right, and although I would never compare mine to his, I can agree, and say this book had a number of influences, supporters and friends. This is the spot for their acknowledgements.

A few years ago, Cody and I went to an overnight paramilitary (cub scouts) camp out at Science World. Later that spring we also went to Camp Byng on the Sunshine Coast. While there they taught us the Kaw Kah Caw bear warning alert. That part is true, my story is fiction. Logan, Shane, Raj and Ned all look like characters from our sojourns, but they are indeed only fictional friends.

A couple of chapters of this book were written while we were in France staying at Carol Shields' house in Burgundy. Carol bought the four hundred year old house with the Pulitzer Prize money awarded to her novel *Stone Diaries*. Carol's daughter, Anne Giardini, gave us the keys. I loved sitting at Carol's desk thinking about her writing. When Anne and Nicholas Giardini published *Startle and Illuminate* I went to a reading where Anne described how her mother emphasized doing good work. However, she stressed it was most important to just "do good, be a good person." Thank you Carol, Anne and Maria.

A few chapters of this book were written while I was at the Yorkmar Writers Retreat in Grays Harbor County, Washington. The Dinnings have always been big supporters of all my novels. There was a time, a long time ago, when we all lived down the road from Timothy Leary.

Three chapters of this book were written when I took a September sojourn to visit friends in Calgary. Norm Zimmer's Coffee Corner provided a great table and desk. Firefighter stories are awfully inspiring. Harry Chapin, in his song *Let Time Go Lightly*, sang, "Old friends mean much more to me because they can see where you are and they know where you've been." Old friends…

Many chapters of this book were written while I sat at my spot on the edge of Mayne Island overlooking the Belle Islets. It is a quiet place to work and wonder.

The epilogue was written when we were staying at my uncle's house in the village of Mehraj in the Punjab. Their support and kindness takes me far.

Ruby Sidhu says, "John, trust the driver." In Ludhiana, her brother Jagtinder, says, "John, double minded drivers are the worst." Nitu drove us all over the Punjab and back again, teaching me many things. Certainly, one thing I know, I will never be able to drive in India.

My cousin Lovely Virk knows how to get things done. Love my cousins.

Walter Larson said, "One Day or Day One—You Decide." Wally and I were co-counselling a young man by the name of Blue Lonechild. Wally encouraged Blue to change some behaviours. Blue heard him, but had trouble listening. Sadly, both have passed on, and are gone too soon. However, their influence lives on in this book.

Julie Eastman reminded me of the *under the stall pal.* Its just fiction in this book, but when I went to Victoria High School, it happened all the time in the boys' second floor washroom.

Psychology has been good to me, yet there have been some tough times along the way. In 1998, I was called to a suburban school where a young man committed suicide because his girlfriend's father had forbidden her to see him anymore. And although I had previously counselled a half dozen or so of these deaths, this was the first where language and culture were big issues to understand. It was a difficult time. I mentioned to my colleague, "Some day I have to write a book about this stuff." She nodded, and said, "Send me a copy."

Sylvia Dudra Pritchard, originally, was a friend of a friend. We met more than a third of a century ago when she was working on a masters degree. I've long lost track of Allan, but have always stayed in touch with Sylvia. She's always been one of the busiest persons I've ever known—especially in retirement. My grandfather, Martin, said, "Johnny, you want to get something done, ask a busy person to do it. Folks who are not busy, there's a reason." Sylvia served as an editor for this book. Sylvia is so kind, lovely, and I appreciate her contribution to this book.

Patti Weiss has read all my novels, and dozens of my psychological assessment reports. She served as an editor for this book as well as *Crazy Cousins*. Patti Weiss really is awfully nice! I am honoured to have such a wonderful friend. Thank you Patti.

Editing my work is not easy. Just ask Beverly Hills scholar, W.A. Harrell, PhD, JD, or preeminent professor, Dr. H. Lee Swanson, University of California Dean, and Distinguished Scholar. And I'm not big name dropping here, way back when, both spent many hours reading my work. However, we all smile recalling the good times. I can't acknowledgement their influence adequately, but it is appreciated.

In the end, I must say in this section: all errors, omissions or mistakes are mine and mine alone.

Vladimir Verano from Third Place Press gave me "Blodfresych"—the Welsh word for cauliflower. It came in handy for this book.

Special thanks to Vladimir—he designed this book as well as my three other novels. Vlad is the best in the business!

Currently, I am working on a new novel—Dr. Randal Reilly travels to the Punjab.

Enid Olive says, it's an awfully long season, and it is too soon to know how this will turn out.

Harbans says, just do what makes you happy.

About the Author

John Carter is a licensed psychologist, an Adjunct Professor at UBC, and a slow paddler off the Mayne Island Coast. *Banny's Boys* is his fourth novel.